All the Things
We Never See

Advance Praise for *All the Things We Never See*

"The stories in Michael Kelly's *All the Things We Never See* balance on the delicate knife edge of the weird, taking place at the moment of incision, just before the blood rushes to the cut. Full of quiet menace and strangeness, with characters bound into odd relationships both to the world and themselves, relationships they themselves often fail to understand, this is weird fiction at is finest."
— Brian Evenson, author of *Song for the Unraveling of the World*

"Michael Kelly's sharp collection of uncanny stories will leave you questioning your relationships, your identity, and reality itself. These stories dig between your ribs and place a cold finger on your heart."
— Paul Tremblay, author of *The Cabin at the End of the World*, and *A Head Full of Ghosts*

"After having nurtured a sterling reputation as a curator of weird fiction, Michael Kelly here reminds us that he's one of its best practitioners, too. *ALL THE THINGS WE NEVER SEE* is eerie and unsettling in the best ways, subverting reality and turning it back on itself, questioning the very earth under your feet. In the end, you're left not scared so much as uncertain, even vulnerable—your throat exposed to unseen forces."
— Nathan Ballingrud, author of *Wounds*, and *North American Lake Monsters*

"Like a cottonmouth sleeping under a silk sheet, there's something unsettling under the surface of Michael Kelly's stories—and once these tales sink their fangs into you, as they did into me, you'll find the venom is strangely addictive."
— Craig Davidson, author of *The Saturday Night Ghost Club*

All the Things We Never See

Michael Kelly

UP UNDERTOW
PUBLICATIONS

Undertow Publications Pickering, ON Canada

undertowpublications.com

Publication History

"Six Haiku", *original to this collection*

"These White Sorrows", *original to this collection*

"One Final Breath", *original to this collection*

"The Face That Looks Back at You" *originally appeared in* Supernatural Tales #18, *2010.*

"The Wounded Bird" *originally appeared in* Murmurations, *Nicholas Royle, ed., 2011.*

"Bait" *originally appeared in* Jamais Vu #1, *2013.*

"A Crack in the Ceiling of the World" *originally appeared in* The New and Perfect Man (Postscripts #24/25), *Nick Gevers & Peter Crowther, eds., 2011.*

"October Dreams" *originally appeared in* Supernatural Tales #22, *2014.*

"Desert of Sharp Sorrows" *originally appeared in* Reflection's Edge, *2007.*

"Blink" *originally appeared in* Tesseracts 16: Parnassus Unbound, *Mark Leslie, ed., 2012.*

"Midnight Carousel" *originally appeared in* Black Petals, Vol. V #2, *2002.*

"Some Other You" *originally appeared in* Shadows Edge, *Simon Strantzas, ed., 2013.*

"Hark at the Wind" *originally appeared in* Space & Time #113, *2011.*

"Other Summers" *originally appeared in* Read Short Fiction, *2013.*

"Another Knife-Grey Day" *originally appeared in* Spectral Realms #2, *2015.*

"Absolution" *originally appeared in* Postscripts to Darkness #4, *2013.*

"All the Things We Never See" *originally appeared in the limited, lettered edition of* Undertow and Other Laments, *2009.*

"Eight Untitled Haiku" *originally appeared in* Whispers from the Shattered Forum #8, *2002.*

"Different Skins" *originally appeared in* Campus Chills, *Mark Leslie, ed., 2009.*

"Tears from an Eyeless Face" *originally appeared in* Supernatural Tales #30, *2015.*

"The White-Face at Dawn" *originally appeared in* A Season in Carcosa, *Joseph S. Pulver Sr., ed., 2012.*

"Turn the Page" *originally appeared in* Black Static #33, *2013.*

"A Guttering of Flickers" *originally appeared in* British Fantasy Society Journal. *2011.*

"Hungry, the Rain-God Awakens" *originally appeared in* Spectral Realms #2, *2015.*

"Conversations with the Dead" *originally appeared in* Unfit for Eden (Postscripts #26/27), *Nick Gevers & Peter Crowther, eds., 2012.*

"The Beach" *originally appeared in* Psycho-Mania!, *Stephen Jones, ed., 2013.*

"Down the Rabbit Hole" *originally appeared in* Nossa Morte #9, *2009.*

"This Red Night" *originally appeared in* Weird Fiction Review, Autumn, *2013.*

"Pieces of Blackness" *originally appeared in* The Grimscribe's Puppets, *Joseph S. Pulver Sr., ed., 2013.*

"A Quiet Axe" *originally appeared in* Nightscript #1, *C.M. Muller, ed., 2015.*

"The Woods" *originally appeared in* Tesseracts 13, *Nancy Kilpatrick & David Morell, eds., 2009.*

For Courtney and Daniel. These stories wouldn't exist without you.

CONTENTS

The Face That Looks Back at You

A storm blows in, frigid and ceaseless.

Such is the anatomy of winter, Alex thinks, peering squint-eyed through the occluded pane of the front door. *If you stare long enough into that white abyss, you'll lose yourself.*

There has been a persistent knocking that has woken him, brought him downstairs to the front door. There are footprints on the doorstep, but no morning newspaper, no neighbours. No one. He thinks he can see the impressions of individual toes in the fresh snow, as if the early morning caller had been barefoot. Impossible, he thinks. The blowing snow has made strange patterns, is all.

Alex hears a rustling sound, and turns to find Teri in her thin nightgown standing at the bottom of the stair landing like some Dickensian apparition. She's shivering, so Alex shuts the door. He sees something in Teri's face. A blankness. She's looking right through him. Her mouth is pulled taffy-wide, almost comically so. Her eyes are broad and unblinking. Her complexion is ice-pale, the colour bleached out like those childhood rubber balls left too long in the sun, all cracked and withered and shrinking in on itself, the life gone out of it. Teri's face seems frozen, and she wears that stretched and worried smile all through the house.

He wonders what Teri would see if she gazed into a mirror. What face would look back at her? Because sometimes, when he looks into a mirror, it's as if he's looking at some past version of himself, a slightly different face that appears to be *off* in a little way. It frightens him, so he avoids mirrors.

Teri is silent, too.

Alex isn't surprised. He figures the strain has finally gotten to her. They have been trying to make a go of it, make things work, but the effort, on both their parts, is not coming to any sort of successful fruition. Theirs is a union, it seems, destined to fail. He isn't sure when it happened. He just woke one day and their relationship, like so many things, was dead.

Therefore, Alex surprises himself somewhat, upon seeing Teri's resigned expression, by suggesting a short road trip up north to the cabin they used to rent back in those early, heady days of love and lazy sex. In addition, he is even more shocked, and pleased, when

Teri's eyes spark briefly and she nods in the affirmative.

It is dead winter, though, and they have only ever vacationed up there in winter once before, and Alex remembers that time as a distinctly unpleasant experience.

Alex calls the resort just the same, and is not at all surprised to learn that yes, indeed, they have a vacancy. Many, in fact. He reserves their regular cabin.

Once they are packed and in the car—the trunk fully loaded and secured—the whole thing seems a decidedly bad decision. The storm has intensified. Icy clumps of snow clot the roads, making the drive treacherous. The car sluices side to side whenever Alex hits the accelerator or the brake. Thankfully, there are no other vehicles on the road. Obviously, Alex thinks, everyone else has more common sense than he does.

Teri sits in the back. Alex thinks it rather odd, but isn't willing to challenge her on it. It is enough that she has agreed to take the trip with him. Once they are there, he figures, everything will sort itself out. Moreover, except for an occasional little whimper, Teri remains mostly silent during the drive. Alex concentrates on keeping the tiny car on the road, and almost forgets he has a passenger until the car swerves and slides and he hears a small moan from the back seat. It is as if he is alone in the car. Occasionally, there is a knocking sound from the trunk, as if something has come loose; a can of pork and beans, perhaps.

In good weather, the drive is 2 hours north, along the coastal highway. They are halfway there now, and it has already taken 2 hours, and to Alex it seems he's been driving this road forever. The road hugs the cliff-face, and Alex clutches the steering wheel white-knuckled. He's surprised, in fact, they haven't closed the road. In summer, this is one of the most scenic routes to take. Now, it is a blinding fog of snow and ice, with another 2 hours, at least, until they reach their destination. Teri sits quietly in the back, staring out the slush-blurred windows. Alex doesn't know how much more of it he can take. Every time he thinks about calling the whole thing off, turning around and finding a spot to stop and ride out the storm, he recalls Teri's face from that morning, that frozen mask, and he keeps his head forward, eyes straight, and doesn't dare look at her, afraid of what will look back at him.

Alex blinks. Tears swim in his vision. His chest hurts, as if his ribs are cracking. And maybe they are. In his head he hears a sharp sound, like thick slabs of ice shattering. He wonders how this fragile vessel of skin and bone can contain his heart—his heart full of love and pain, full to bursting. We weren't meant for this, he thinks. So much love. And pain. It'll be the death of us. Sometimes he thinks he should open himself up, just a little, and let some of that love and pain leak out. Relieve the pressure.

It is his fault, he knows. How could he have not seen it? He loves her so much, and yet each new day she appears more with-drawn, her face growing ever sadder, collapsing in on itself, her mood sombre and indifferent. Slowly, she is disappearing, vanishing, becoming something else, someone else. He has a momentary vision of glancing into the back of the car, and despite the furious flurry of white outside, it is dark in the back seat, like a deep and ancient hole, and he doesn't see Teri, so a brief panic flares up in him and he blinks, leans over, and there she is pulling herself up the back of the seat, and her face leers over the top and she stares back at him, grinning blackly.

The vision passes and he is still moving forward, but the car is in the wrong lane. He pulls the wheel, over-correcting, and the vehicle slides across the lanes onto the shoulder, but he corrects and gets them into the proper lane. Teri sighs heavily, as if she's been holding her breath.

"It's okay," Alex says. "I've got it under control." *What*, he thinks. *What do I have under control?* A chill black wave flows through him. He has the sense he's drowning.

He wipes a hand over his wet eyes. He fights the road, fights his feelings, and fights the urge to pull over onto the icy shoulder. Instead, he does what he always does, and pushes forward.

Then Teri's breath is beside him, in his ear, harsh and cold. "I have to pee," she says. Alex thinks it comical and laughs.

"Really," Teri pleads. Then, quieter, "Sorry." And Alex gets the impression she's apologizing for something else entirely. As if she was to blame for the whole imbroglio.

Alex steers across the empty oncoming lane and pulls the jittering car safely onto the shoulder. He leaves the engine running. He doesn't want to take any chances that it won't start up again and they'll be stuck in this frozen nightmare. He peers out the side window. A lone tree stands in the fields of white, limbs like bones reaching for the sky.

"Okay," Alex says.

"Out *there?*" Teri asks.

Alex doesn't turn around, just continues to stare out the ice-cracked window at the stark tableaux. He sighs. "Where else, Ter? You can't go in here. You can squat behind the car. No one will see. Christ, there's no one else around. No one."

There's a whispery sound from the back seat. "The tree," she says. "I'll go behind the tree. Just in case."

He drums on the steering wheel. "Suit yourself."

The rear door opens and a blast of icy air roars into the car. Then the door slams shut and Alex yells "Be careful," but the sudden silence swallows his words, as if he has no voice at all. Too late, always too late. He can see Teri trudging toward the tree, but she doesn't seem to be making any progress. Minutes tick by and she's the same dark smudge hobbling away, frozen in a different time. Then he blinks and she's gone.

A couple more hours, Alex thinks, and then we can start a fire, start a meal, and start anew.

Alex shifts in his seat. The car is getting stuffy. He blinks, nods forward. Tired. So tired. Of everything.

His eyes snap open, startled, confused. For a brief, terrible moment he doesn't know where he is, then he remembers. He'd nodded off in the car waiting for Teri.

Teri!

Alex turns, looks into the back seat. It's dark and empty. He thinks he hears something in the trunk, a scratching and banging sound, strange thumping, but that's impossible because there's nothing in the trunk that could make those sounds.

Where is Teri? he thinks. Surely she should be back by now. He hadn't really fallen asleep, had he? Alex rubs the window, squints into the distance. Nothing. A world of swirling white.

He steps from the car, careful not to lock the door behind him. The wind and snow sting his face. Suddenly his bladder is a sharp pain, so he unzips and urinates on the icy shoulder of road. Then he hugs himself, puts his head down, and trundles off toward the tree. He looks, but cannot find any of Teri's tracks in the snow. He figures the storm has quickly covered them over, almost as if they never existed. Storms, whether literal or metaphorical, could do that, he knew.

Alex reaches the tree sooner than he expects. It wasn't as far away as he'd thought. A trick of the wan, winter light. But Teri is nowhere to be seen. A cold ache seeps into Alex, hugs his chest and heart, like a contracting band. His whole body may crack and split into red shards.

"Teri!," he yells, but the winter wind takes his voice and pulls it apart like smoke. And despite the incessant mournful wind, Alex thinks he hears a knocking sound. He whirls, and he's misjudged the distance of the tree completely, as the car is only a stone's throw away, and he can see something through the rear window, a hand pressed against the frosted glass, fingers splayed. Teri! And the band around his chest loosens. Then her face, murky behind the fogged pane, looms into view. Her fingers curl into a fist and she starts to bang slow against the window. Alex smiles, trots back to the car. But the door won't budge, it's jammed, so he knocks on the window. *Knock-knock.* Then the door gives and he stumbles into the front seat.

Alex sits, catches his breath. Without turning he asks, "Where were you?"

"Here," she says. "Always here. Waiting. You took quite a while."

"Sorry," he says.

"Where were you?"

Alex looks into the white abyss, gestures. "Out there," he says.

"Don't leave me, Alex. Don't ever leave me."

He looks up, into the rear-view mirror, but all he sees is blackness. *Why is it so damn dark in here?* he thinks. Then he hears her back there, crying quietly.

"Ter," Alex says, "why don't you come up front with me?"

"I… I don't want you to see me," she says. "Not like this. It's okay. I like it in here in the quiet, in the dark."

Alex nods, pulls the car back onto the road. The storm has let up, though the day is still grey, a damp mist smothering everything. He drives into the greying day. The fog pushes against the car, making the headlights ineffectual. Teri is silent, so he turns on the radio. At first there's nothing but cold, black static, then he finds a station playing eighties pop music and he settles in. In the back, Teri hums, and an hour later they are pulling up the long and twisting road into the resort.

There are no other vehicles in sight. Alex pulls around to the back, where their cabin borders the lake. The key has been left in a little lock box, to which they've been given the combination.

In the cabin, Teri brightens. "Look," she says, pointing. "A ship's trunk. How quaint. I had one as a child, in the attic."

They move across the tiny room to the old trunk. It is black and battered and fully three feet tall. A tarnished gold and leather hasp keeps the lid closed. Teri bends to the hasp, pulls the bolt free.

Suddenly Alex doesn't want the lid opened, doesn't want to see what's inside. "Wait," he says, grabbing her arm.

Teri stares at him, puzzled. "What?"

"There might be something in there, Ter."

"Of course," she says. "That's what they are for. What's the worst it could be?"

Yes, he thinks, *what's the worst it could be?* He doesn't answer, just looks away as the lid creaks open.

Teri laughs. "See, you daft bugger, nothing to worry about."

Alex glances down. The box is dark and empty. Then Teri is climbing over the edge and into the trunk.

"Ter, please, what are you doing? Get out of there."

Teri sits in the dark box, stares up at Alex wide-eyed. "Don't worry, it's okay." She shifts and Alex thinks her face shifts, too, ripples in the darkness. And when she speaks again, her voice is changed. Huskier. Breathy.

"When I was very young, Alex, before Mom and Dad split up, I'd hear them downstairs arguing, fighting. Their voices would carry up the heating grates. They would say awful things to each other. Just awful.

"I would cover my ears, hide under my pillow or my bedcovers to try and escape the noise. One day, while they were having a particularly vicious argument, I found a stepladder and climbed up into the attic. There I saw the trunk, just like this one, Alex. Black and old and timeworn. I went to the trunk, opened the lid, and peered in.

"A face looked back at me."

Alex shivers. He's taken aback by how suddenly talkative she's become, this reversal of roles.

"I was startled," Teri continues. "A small shriek escaped me, but the fight downstairs raged on, and no one heard me. Steeling myself, I crept to the box, and peeked over the edge. There were many faces in the box, in fact. And colourful costumes. They were masks, you see. Plastic and rubber, some with feathers and sequins. There were capes and gowns and hats. It was a costume trunk.

"So I played dress-up. I could become someone else. We all do, eventually, anyway.

"I was a queen, a witch, and a trickster. Even a burlesque dancer. But while I was playing, something happened. The house grew still. The fighting downstairs had stopped. I listened. I heard footsteps below me."

Teri reaches out from the dark space and grips Alex's hand.

"Suddenly, I was afraid, Alex. Those footsteps... the silence of the house... nothing seemed natural. So, I crawled into the trunk, closed the lid and waited. It was dark and silent, and my heart beat so hard and so fast that I felt surely that whoever was downstairs searching for me—and I knew, somehow, that they were looking for *me*—would hear it and come up the ladder into the attic."

Alex shuffles. "Jesus, Ter, what happened?"

"I waited. And waited. I was scared. I'd left the ladder below the attic door, so I knew it was only a matter of time before someone would come to look for me. I thought, perhaps, they wouldn't check the trunk, but I'd left the costumes strewn around, so it'd be the obvious place to look. Eventually I heard a voice calling, *Teri, Teri*. It sounded a bit like my mom's voice, but at the same time it sounded like someone else. I heard a creak from the attic trusses, and I held my breath. Then the lid opened, and I blinked wildly, and someone wearing my mom's face was staring down at me smiling. 'What are you doing?' she asked.

"'Waiting for my mom,' I answered.

"My not-Mom's smile grew wider. 'I *am* your mom, silly girl. Come out of there.'

"Then she reached in for me and I saw the blood on her hands."

Alex kneels beside the trunk. "Why didn't you tell me this before now?"

Teri blinks. "I don't know. It's as if it happened to someone else, some other me.

"Staring up at the woman with the bloody hands, I saw, somewhere beneath the surface, my mom behind that flesh and blood mask. This was my mom now. She'd changed irrevocably, somehow. She was pretending to be someone else. And I decided it wasn't much different from playing dress-up.

"She gently pulled me from the trunk. We washed up together, then had milk and cookies, like a real family. She told me 'Your father's gone, dear. I'm sorry.'"

Teri shakes. Tears roll down her pale cheeks. Her hand squeezes Alex's arm. "I couldn't bear it if you were to leave, too, Alex," she says.

Alex stands, helps her from the chest. They move over to the small couch. He pulls the afghan from the couch and wraps it around them. For a long time they hold each other. They do not speak. The cabin is quiet and still. Outside, the wind sings a song of ice.

It is morning. Alex is at the cabin door. There'd been a persistent knocking that had woken him. He glances at Teri. She is still on the couch, scrunched child-like under the covering, at peace.

He wipes a hand across the small window pane, peers outside. It is like looking through a glassine envelope. Alex shoves his feet into his boots, throws his coat on, carefully opens the door and steps outside.

Raw daylight makes him blink. He squints left and right. There is no one, nothing that can account for the knocking. The lake is a black mirror with spots of dusted snow. Alex thumps down the steps and moves toward the lake. A lone black bird soars in a grey wedge of sky. He smiles, thinks about sweet Teri and her sad story, thinks that he might burst in this sudden new world of infinite and crystalline possibilities.

Alex steps onto the frozen lake. As a child he skated on a frozen pond near his home. It was a time of pure innocence and exuberance. Flush with new love, and needing to release some of it, Alex pushes forward, onto the surface, booted feet mimicking his skating moves from yesteryear. His heart is a wild thing, thumping. His chest hurts, and there is a sharp snap, as if his ribs have split and broken and his heart might just escape. Then another loud crack, an explosion of ice, and a fissure opens on the lake. Black water bubbles up. A long seam runs along the top of the frozen lake. The fissure widens, splits, and a slab of ice tilts, tosses Alex forward, pitches him into the cold, black depths.

The cold envelops him, seeps into him, becomes part of him. *Cold*, he thinks. *So cold.* And *Teri*.

He is under the ice, floating, a gentle current slowly carrying him further out. A strange peace washes through him. He can see through the ice, a window to the real world, he thinks. Not a mirror for the changing sorrows of our faces, but a window. A black bird, perhaps the same one, circles in the brightening sky. He tries to smile, but cannot.

I love you, Teri.

Alex waits. His eyes are wide and unblinking. He hears her, calling his name, coming across the ice. Above him, Teri's face swims into his vision, and he warms, his heart beats once, twice. He tries to open his mouth, but cannot. Tries to move his arms and legs, but cannot. He cannot catch a breath. He cannot even blink, to let her know that he is fine; he is going to be all right. His face is a frozen mask.

Teri is pounding on the thick ice with a closed fist. Her face twists in agony, her mouth moving, and though Alex knows he should not be able to hear her, he is somehow able to make out what she is saying: *Don't leave me, Alex. Don't ever leave me.*

I won't, Alex thinks, as his vision fades and blackens, and a dark and cold stillness permeates him.

Sometime later Alex is on the frozen lake, staring across the icy expanse at the cabin. The winter wind gusts across the frozen water, but he isn't cold. Alex doesn't feel anything. He moves across the glassy expanse effortlessly, as if skating. There are tracks on the ice, footprints, and he can discern toes, and he wonders what would compel someone to go barefoot across the ice.

Alex follows the footprints to the small cabin.

Teri.

He doesn't remember opening the door, but he's inside the cabin now. Teri is nowhere to be seen, as if she's somehow vanished, because, he knows, she's been vanishing for a very long time, changing, becoming someone else, but he hears a steady knocking—*knock... knock... knock...* —coming from the large trunk, and he glides across the room to the heavy black box and lifts the lid.

Teri is in the deep trunk, curled tightly, barefoot, arms hugging her knees, rocking forward and back, forward and back, *knock-knock,* her head smashing the trunk's inner wall.

Alex leans down, smiles. *It's okay, Ter. I'm here. I won't leave. Ever.*

Teri is in the car now, and she's thinking that this is the point where the engine won't turn over and she will be stuck in this frozen wasteland for all eternity, but she turns the key and the engine purrs to life and she drives blindly into a new winter storm.

She doesn't dare turn around and look into the back seat, too afraid of whose face she might see.

The Wounded Bird

The man is old, infirm.

The man is lonely.

He hasn't always been old, or infirm, but he's always been lonely.

The man is sitting in his favourite chair, drinking tea, when he hears a small thump. He eases himself up, and totters over to the window, peers outside. He sees something small and red in the grass. A ball, perhaps. He goes out to investigate and finds that it is a bird on the ground. The bird is alive. The bird cannot fly. The bird hops and stutters and falls. Hops, stutters, falls again.

Maybe it's an old bird, the man thinks. Blind.

Maybe it's lonely.

The man lifts the bird, holds it. He has never before held a living thing in his hands. He brings the bird inside.

The man puts the bird in a cardboard box lined with tissue. He gazes admiringly at the bird in the box. It is a beautiful bird: red like his heart. He puts a lid on the box and punches breathing holes in it. Then he sits in his chair, thinking, sipping tepid tea.

The bird is quiet.

The man is quiet.

Then, from the box, comes a low metallic sound, a *chit chit*.

And the man smiles, happy that he isn't so old that he can't hear. Happy that he is no longer lonely.

But the man doesn't know anything about birds, so he gathers his coat and his cane and he takes the subway to the library. He gets a library card. He borrows books about birds. He even buys a book-bag so he can tote the books home. He sits on the subway and looks at the other passengers. The man feels good.

At home the man goes straight to the box and lifts the lid. He looks at the bird. The bird, unblinking, looks at the man. It is a beautiful bird, the man thinks. Red, like his blood.

The man reads the books. He learns that the bird is a Northern Cardinal. It is a male. It is a song bird. *Chit chit* it sings, and *purdy purdy purdy*. He loves the sound of its song.

That night, the man sleeps on the sofa next to the cardboard box. He keeps a table lamp on, so the bird will have some light. In the fitful night he thinks he hears rustling and a soft, insistent thumping sound.

When he wakes, the man goes straight to the box and lifts the lid. The bird flies out, past the surprised man. It hits the window, falls. The man gasps, reaches for the bird, but it rouses itself and flies away before he can reach it. The bird circles overhead, round and round, a red ring, before landing on the edge of the cardboard box. Quickly, the man snaps the lid back on the box, trapping the bird.

The bird is quiet.

The man is panting.

Then the man has an idea. There is a pet store 2 blocks away. He walks to the pet store. He doesn't even bring his cane. He buys bird food—seed, grains, insects. He buys a cage.

The man sets up the bird cage. He could not carry a large cage, but it has a perch and a feeder. He lifts the lid on the box just a little. He puts his hand in, feels around blindly, then snatches the bird. He puts the bird in the cage.

The man fills the bird feeder, stares at the bird, smiles. Again he thinks about what a beautiful bird it is. Red. Like his love.

The bird stutters along the bottom of the cage. *Chit chit. Chit chit.* The bird is talkative in its cage: *chit chit purdy chit chit purdy.* The man even thinks he can hear another songbird outside his window, as if in answer.

For many days the bird is talkative and busy. It launches from the perch and hits the cage, chattering, wings fluttering. The cage shakes. The man feels hurt. He tries to soothe the bird. He coos to it, placating. After a time, the bird is quiet. It rests on its perch, silent and unblinking. The man smiles.

In the following weeks the man talks to the bird, tells it he loves it. He reads to the bird. He plays music for the bird—Debussy. But the bird remains silent and songless. The man feels his heart breaking.

Then one day the man goes to sleep and something opens up inside of him, something red, and he doesn't wake.

The house becomes silent. Dark. It stays silent and dark for some while, then there is a *chit-chitting* in the dark. *Chit chit. Chit*

chit. And the bird continues its chatter for some days. *Chit-chit*. But the house is silent except for the bird's insistent cry.

Then, after some time, the bird is quiet.

Bait

Father was dead, and mother was missing.

That summer, the world was small and grey. Seeley Cove was a tiny, remote fishing village on the east coast, perpetually grey; fog and misty tendrils clinging to everything. The cove's small harbour was a whirlpool of choppy dark water under a sky like bleached sackcloth. Houses and shacks ringed the inlet, wooden boards scoured to the colour of brittle bone by the ceaseless salt air. The structures listed, too, as if the land beneath had shifted. From the bay, as you travelled by boat back to the wharf, the rickety shacks resembled rows of rotted teeth in a diseased mouth.

I was thirteen years old when I came to live in Seeley Cove. I'd been to the cove once before, with my father, for a day of fishing. This was mere days after my mother had left us. My dad's brother, Ivar, lived in the cove and had a fishing boat. It was a bright clear day. Gulls wheeled and cried in a cloudless, blue sky. The water was calm and glass-green. I remember my dad and uncle pulling beers from a cooler, smiling, and laughing. With mother gone, how could father laugh and smile, I thought.

I remember my dad throwing bait into the water. He'd reach into a plastic bin and shovel a meaty soup into the sea. The gulls squawked, dived, and gorged on the bait. I don't remember catching any fish. We ate steak that night.

I brooded that whole weekend, trying to make sense of my mother's disappearing act. I recall Ivar trying to cheer me up, winking, telling me that we were going to catch a mermaid. And I remember Ivar's four-fingered hand. His right hand had no pinkie finger, just a scarred and nubby protuberance, livid white, that wriggled like a maggot.

After my father's funeral, Uncle Ivar drove me back to his house in the cove to stay with him. "For the time being," he said then. With my mother's whereabouts unknown, and no other living family, Family and Social Services allowed this arrangement until they could place me with a foster family.

It was springtime, cold, winter clutching us still in its icy embrace. Ivar wore an ill-fitting suit, and smelled of fish and gasoline. He smiled a lot, but it wasn't a quick and easy smile. It was slow, deliberate. During the three-hour drive to his house, he talked about the war overseas. I don't remember which war. There was always a war overseas.

The cove was dying back then. It's dead now, but at that time, it was in its final throes. They still fished cod, but the stocks were increasingly dwindling. Those who were young enough moved inland, found new jobs. If they didn't find jobs, they didn't come back. There were diversions in the cities. Better to be unemployed there than in the cove, where the main entertainment was the Friday night Ceilidh in Ruth McGonnagal's house.

Uncle Ivar's house was grey and dreary and wind-burned, like Ivar. The house was a square two-storey, dry and brittle despite the perpetual fog-shrouded basin. There was a living room, a kitchen, and dining room. A staircase bisected the house right down the middle. Upstairs was a bathroom and two bedrooms. The bedroom I was given was decorated in lace and pastels. "The guest room," Ivar said. What kind of guests, I wondered?

At the back of the house, there was a small cut-out and three concrete steps that led down to a padlocked metal door. A cellar of some sort. I asked uncle Ivar about the cellar. His eyes clouded for a moment, and then he smiled, clapped me on the back with his meaty, four-fingered hand. "Workshop," he said. "Tools. You not go in there. Not safe."

Ivar still fished, seasonally. When I came to Seeley Cove, he would take me down to the wharf on weekends and take his old fishing trawler out for a cruise around the bay. Fishing season was still a few weeks away, so we'd just circle the inlet, the briny sea air making me giddy and faint. "Later," Ivar said. "Later we'll go farther." 'Farther' sounded like 'father.'

Father.

Mother.

Both gone.

The boat was squat and solid. He showed me the engine and the nets, tangled in seaweed. Showed me the winches that lowered and lifted the heavy netting. I wondered how it would feel trapped in those heavy ropes. Wondered if Ivar still dreamed of catching a mermaid. Were fish aware that they were caught, trapped? Or does the realisation only come when dragged, mouths gasping, out of their watery home?

Ivar allowed me to take the steering wheel and the throttle. He let me operate the winch, a metal contraption of open gears and cogs that I was careful to keep my hands clear of. I imagined the gears chewing Ivar's ragged pinkie finger. It didn't look safe. How could it be any safer than his off-limits workshop?

That locked door struck a nerve.

Each day that Spring, after the ancient orange school bus dropped me off, I'd stop at Ivar's locked back door. Sometimes I'd rattle the padlock. Once, I thought I heard noises from inside, a strange breathy sound, like a sigh, and a tapping, but it was just the echo of the lock knocking against the door.

Ivar was a good cook. He made stews and soups, pastas, meat pies. Simple, tasty food. There must have been a freezer in that cellar, because he'd go out, walk past the side window, a dark blur, then I'd hear the telltale creak of a door slowly opening. Moments later, he'd return and place several packets of meat wrapped in butcher's paper in the refrigerator.

"What is it?" I once asked.

He stopped, looked at me, looked at the bloody packet in his hand, as if considering. "Moose," he said. "Deer."

"Which?" I asked.

That slow smile of his inched across his mouth. He just shrugged his shoulders. "It not matter. Is good."

I'd never seen Ivar hunt. And I'd never seen where he kept the key to the cellar door.

At dinner one night, hunched over a spicy stew, I asked Ivar where he got the meat.

Ivar blinked. He pointed at me, cocked his thumb like a gun, and pulled a pretend trigger. "Hunting," he said. "In winter. No fish."

"Is it hard," I asked, "shooting something? Killing something?"

"Is easy," Ivar said. "Too easy. You just need right lure."

"Lure?"

He scratched a cheek, grinned. "Bait."

"What kind of bait?" I asked.

His grin vanished. He appeared thoughtful for a moment. "Anything," he said. "You are hungry, you eat. No?"

I nodded.

That wide, dumb grin crept back. "I like meat," he said.

We ate moose, lamb, chicken, venison. Fish, too. Mostly cod.

School was a drear existence. So close to the end of the school year it was hard to make friends. And I didn't. I didn't try, and neither did my classmates. I was the kid whose dad had blown his face off. No one would come near me. As if I had some sickness they might catch. Bad luck, perhaps. I was a pariah.

In late spring, fishing season opened. I'd come home from school, do my homework, read or listen to music—Ivar didn't own a television—then he'd get back around suppertime, prepare the meal, and we'd eat. If Ivar wasn't complaining about a war overseas, he was complaining about that day's catch. "No good," he'd mutter. "No good. Greed killed them. Greed."

"The fish?" I'd asked him.

Ivar stared at me. "Greed kills everything."

One day near the end of the school year, I trudged home from the bus stop to find Ivar's ancient Ford pick-up in the gravel driveway. He was home early. Inside, I heard noises upstairs. Voices. Giggling. I started up the stairs, then stopped. I went quietly to the kitchen. I opened cupboards, looked inside, went to the refrigerator, poked my head in, not knowing what I was looking for or what I wanted. There was milk, pickles, butter, and packets of meat and fish. More laughter from upstairs. I went to the tiny kitchen table, pulled out a chair and sat. Minutes later, Ivar came into the kitchen. It was hard to read his expression. I stood. "I was just going out," I said. "To play."

"Good," Ivar said. "Is good. You go."

I left the house and walked down to the village proper. The streets were hilly and serpentine, like a maze. A crystalline mist clung to everything. Nothing stirred, as if the world, or at least this town, were an ancient fossil trapped in amber.

Hours later, I returned. Ivar was at the table, eating. His face and hands were scrubbed pink, as if he'd just showered. A toothsome smile spread slowly across his face. He kicked a chair out from under the table. "Sit now," he said. "Eat." I sat and ate, then, when Ivar retired to the other room to listen to Chopin, I went upstairs to do my homework and to read. The room, with its lace and pastels, was suffocating.

"What happened to your finger?" I asked.

It was a Saturday, early July. School was out for the year. I was whittling at a piece of wood with a jackknife. I was handy with a knife. Ivar was sitting in a lawn chair, nursing a quart bottle of beer, staring down towards the dark water of the bay as if he hadn't heard me.

"Your finger," I said, "was it an accident?"

Ivar regarded me. "No," he said. He took a long pull from the bottle. "No accident."

I stared at him, blinked.

"Bait," he said. "Lure." He put the beer down on a small table beside the chair, then stood and went into the house. He returned with a long knife, and a raw carrot. He placed the carrot on the table then swiftly chopped down. The knife bit into the carrot, and Ivar sawed it into two pieces. He threw one-half of the carrot towards me. It landed in the dirt beside my marbles. "Eat," he said.

I blinked again. Ivar looked at me impassively, then quieter this time, he repeated, "eat."

I picked up the ragged carrot, brushed it off, threw it into my mouth and chewed.

Ivar waved his four-fingered hand at me. "Meat. Bait. Sometimes you need meat to catch meat."

Solemnly, I chewed the carrot, gulped.

"You're hungry, you eat," said Ivar. "No?"

I nodded.

"War," Ivar said. He fidgeted with his beer bottle, looked to the ground, then again, softer. "The war."

I stood, and went inside, up to my room. I looked out the bedroom window. Ivar sat in the chair, holding the beer bottle, staring down to the water. I lay down on my bed, gazed up at the bare ceiling. The bed began to spin. The carrot was a hard and sour thing in my stomach. It came up with the remains of that day's breakfast.

That night I dreamt of teeth crunching bone, and sounds, taps and sighs, coming from the locked cellar.

Sometimes during that grey and cheerless summer Ivar would take me out on his boat for the day's fishing. When we'd cruise past the harbour he'd give me the wheel and I'd guide us out to the wide ocean. Ivar told me to follow the gulls. "The birds are smart," he said. "They find the fish." It put me in mind of that first fishing trip, dad and Ivar smiling, drinking. The gulls overhead, shrieking. They talked quietly about mom. They didn't seem to miss her as much as I did.

We would lower the nets and drag them, pulling up seaweed and struggling, gasping cod. There'd always be a couple dozen cod, but Ivar was always displeased. "Too young," he'd say. "Too small." And he'd throw half of them back. I was secretly happy for the ones who escaped.

As the summer wore on, Ivar became increasingly sullen and withdrawn. He'd come back each night agitated, and even less communicative than usual. Some nights he'd get in his pick-up and leave, returning late. And some nights he'd spend hours in the cellar.

One night, I asked Ivar about my father. "Why? Why did he do it?"

A curious expression crossed Ivar's face. He put down his soupspoon. "Do what?" he asked.

"Kill himself."

"Weak," Ivar said. "He was weak."

"But *why?*" I implored.

Ivar glared at me. "Some things best you not know. Some things best kept secret."

Then he quietened and wouldn't talk further about my father, despite my protestations. I wanted to hear about mother, father, even the war. Ivar just glowered at me. He finished his soup in silence, then grabbed his coat and left the house. I heard the truck start up and then pull away.

One day midweek, midsummer, Ivar brought home another lady guest. She wasn't young, but she wasn't old. She wore cut-off jeans and a red halter top. She smiled at me and I saw that she was pretty. Her legs were long and tanned, and when I looked at them something stirred in me, a spreading warmth, a tingling. Ivar was smiling. Did he feel that same strange tingling? She had a tattoo on her ankle, a woman with a fish tail. Ivar had netted his mermaid. I wondered how he lured her, what he used for bait.

I was staring at the tattoo.

"You like?" she asked me.

I gulped, looked away, and muttered "Yes."

Ivar glared at me, unblinking. I trudged out the front door and away from the house.

Hours later I returned to the empty house, silent except for the plaintive wail of the sea wind that shook the frame.

In the following days Ivar was in a decidedly pleasant mood, almost gregarious. He cooked, and we ate. He didn't complain about the fishing, didn't complain about the war overseas. He was, for a change, quick with a smile. After dinner he'd go into the living room, sit and listen to Chopin or Mozart, and nurse quart bottles of Molson Stock Ale.

One night I came down to find him dozing in a chair, snoring, several empty beer bottles stacked on the end table.

I tiptoed to the table, stopped and watched Ivar for several minutes. He didn't move, just snored. Carefully, I plucked the keys from the table-top and snuck outside. I went around the back, to the cellar door. I fumbled with the keys in the dark but found the one that opened the lock. I pushed the door open gently, and crept inside. I pawed at the wall for a light switch, and then flipped it up.

The room was large, grey, and industrial. In the centre of the space was a large table-saw with a massive ragged-toothed blade jutting up from the middle of it. To the left was a deep sink and a faucet with a green nylon hose. Beside the sink was a wooden work-bench. The far wall held a number of instruments: hammers, pliers, screwdrivers, knives, and saws. I moved to the wall, lifted a knife from the pegboard. It was thin and sharp, a boning knife. I turned.

A large black-plastic pail sat in a corner. To the right was a recessed floor with a drain. Several large, curved hooks hung above the drain. I pictured large carcasses hanging from those hooks—moose and deer—their dumb, dead eyes staring. A long white freezer was pushed against a side wall.

A "workshop" Ivar had called it. There was no wood or sawdust evident. No mechanical parts or engines.

The shop was clean, organized. The tools hung in neat rows. The floor was spotless; the workbench empty. That tidiness sent a shiver through me.

I stared at the freezer. The room tilted. Everything seemed to slow; my heart, my blood, my thoughts. I shuffled over to the freezer, stared at the gleaming white surface and the silvered handle. I was trembling. I grasped the handle and lifted the freezer's lid.

Meat. Packets of meat wrapped in brown paper, like the packages in the refrigerator, dated and labelled, 'moose,' 'venison,' and sealed in clear plastic bags.

I let out a breath and closed the lid. Then I panicked. What if Ivar woke? What if he found me down here? Turning, I switched off the light, left the cellar, and returned, quietly to the house.

Ivar was still in the chair, sleeping. I moved to the table, placed the key ring down slowly, hoping it wouldn't jangle. Ivar's hand shot out, grabbed my wrist. His eyes opened, sleepily, like something awakened from an ancient slumber. His hand, tight on my wrist, missing a pinkie, felt alien.

I yanked my wrist free, made a show of gathering the empty beer bottles. "I'm tidying up," I said. There was a tremor to my voice.

Ivar's calculated smile appeared. "Tidy, yes," he said. "Is good to be clean. Neat. No messes." Then his eyes fluttered closed and he seemed to doze off.

I took the bottles into the kitchen, put them in the case. Then I went upstairs, crawled into bed and stared at the ceiling for hours, my head swimming and stomach churning.

At breakfast the next morning I had no appetite. I nibbled at some dry toast but left the runny eggs and greasy bacon untouched. I could barely stand to look at my plate. Could barely stand to look at Ivar.

"Today you'll fish," Ivar said. "No?"

He showed no apparent ill-effects from the previous night's drinking. He was staring at me, waiting for an answer.

"No," I said.

"Today you'll fish," he repeated, then pulled my plate across the table and forked egg into his mouth.

After breakfast we climbed into his pick-up and headed to the wharf. There was a large plastic black bin in the truck's bed. Just like the pail I'd seen in the corner of his workshop.

At the dock he wheeled the bin down to the boat and loaded it onto the deck.

"I want the wheel," I said.

Ivar nodded. I started the engine, took the wheel, and eased us out of the small bay. Behind me, the curved inlet was a brown and grey mouth, screaming. Once past the dock I pushed the throttle forward and headed to open water.

Wind and salt air. Grey clouds scudding across a rumpled obsidian sky. The boat speeding toward the horizon. My eyes wet.

I slowed the boat, killed the engine, left the wheel and moved to the deck.

"This it then?" Ivar said.

I wiped a hand across my face, took a deep breath.

Ivar hauled a shovel over to the black bin and lifted the lid off. "Bait," he said.

Overhead, gulls cried.

I watched as Ivar scooped the soupy red mess overboard. I half expected to see a hank of hair, or a piece of pale skin with a mermaid tattoo. But I didn't. Just a red mess.

Then I was moving toward Ivar, the boning knife in my hand. I was crying, shrieking like the grey gulls. And Ivar turned toward the sound, brought his head around, and I stepped behind him, quickly, as a grimace briefly crossed his face, and I grabbed his hair, pulled his head back as he dropped the shovel and swatted at me, then I drew that thin, sharp blade straight across his neck.

He fell to the ground then, clutching at his neck as a red mist pulsed from his throat. He kicked and twitched and flopped. His mouth gasped, like a fish, and I decided it really wasn't that different.

After a while it was over, and I manoeuvred him overboard. Still the gulls squawked. I dumped the bin over, as well. I cleaned the deck, turned the boat around and steered it back towards Seeley Cove, back toward that fetid brown mouth. The wind made my eyes tear up.

Ivar was right, it is easy to kill something. Too easy. You just need the right bait.

Six Haiku

The Starry Rift

Birthed—starry blackness
I float, tethered to this
cosmic umbilicus

Puppet March

Wooden battle march
Snickering bayonet song
Dead marionettes

Ishmael, Alone

Adrift in green sea
he weeps and sleeps and dreams of
white leviathan

Halloween

Crisp dead leaves scuttle,
children caper and cackle
with witch's laughter

Dawn Raid

Sky full of space ships—
tumbleweeds in a ghost town
The war of all worlds

Something Fishy

The Old Ones beckon
Something stirs in piscine depths
Sinister something

A Crack in the Ceiling of the World

There's a crack in the ceiling of this world, and Ezekiel will find it before he is dead. He is the last of his kind. He hasn't seen anyone in a very long time. There's no one else. He's seen the bodies, the remains, scattered along the empty railways, left so long that the bones are pulverized gravel. He imagines more bodies at the bottom of the pits, stacked like kindling, fading to fine dust, dead and gone like ghosts and memories. Long ago, when scorched air blew up from the furnace below, Ezekiel imagined it was fuel from the dead. Now he knew it to be true.

The passage is blocked. Ezekiel climbs out of the battered tram. The tram is ancient. It's taken him as far as it can. He trundles off into the dark, following the rails that curve ever upward. Ezekiel rode this rail line once before, on his long descent.

Maybe they're not all dead, Ezekiel thinks. Maybe some heard the old tales and found the crack in the world and made it to the outer world. Knowing would be enough.

Jane would soon be dead.

There was a sudden loud crack in the world, and she thought everyone might be dead.

It was 8:46 a.m. and she'd settled at her desk when there was a rib-rattling explosion. The framed photo of Chloe, her daughter, fell to the floor, splintering into a glassy web. Through the office windows the blue sky gave way to a storm of dark, flaming debris, then dust, then silence. Jane thought the hush was worse than the clamour. The din of chaos afforded opportunities. There was no hope in silence.

The PA system announced an evacuation, something about the North Tower. Jane scooped up the photo of Chloe and ran to the elevators. She hugged the photo to her chest and rode the jittery elevator with a crush of pale, quaking people to the lobby. Jane sprinted across the lobby to the subway entrance. If she could make it to the N/R train, she could get home to Chloe.

She'd reached the subway concourse at precisely 9:03 a.m. when there was another blast, angrier than the first.

The sky cracked and fell.

This was once the realm of memories. Memories were king. Memories were true. Deep in the bowels of this world, in the lightless mines, memories were all you had. Soon enough, even your memories succumbed to the terrible heat of the blast furnaces, the infernal machines that scorched everything.

When he was very young Ezekiel had heard his father's father speak in an ancient wavering voice about another world. It existed far up beyond the uppermost sections, past the dust-stiff trolleys and rusted rails, past the quarries of hand-hewn rock; past the now dormant furnaces; beyond, even, the heavy wrought-iron gates that kept everything in, kept everything out.

It was a place of light and water and soft earth.

Alone, in the stone silence of this world, Ezekiel had started his ascent. He'd rode on the back of a dying dragon, faint heat drafts from below pushing man and dragon upward. He'd pulled himself up quarry walls, bloodied hands and feet groping for purchase on crumbling, fire-weakened cliff face. He'd clambered over dusty trolley cars; manoeuvred along labyrinthine passageways and cob-webbed catacombs; crawled through twisting tunnels; rode an ancient tram along a steep road of rails to the ceiling of the world.

Now, broken rock is heaped in the dim passageway. Muffled noise reaches Ezekiel. He smiles. So close. He shuffles forward, climbs atop the broken concrete. Beyond the rock wall is a thin seam of light.

The crack in the ceiling of the world.

Ezekiel scrambles up the rocky incline and hurries forward. A blast rocks him, sends him sprawling. *God's hammer*, he thinks. Bright light flares and crackles in the seam. A mist of grey dust pushes through the crack. Ezekiel crawls to the fissure. He stands and steps through into the other world.

Jane dreamed of steel dragons descending from high aeries, swooping from soot-choked skies to smash into skyscrapers...

She opened her eyes to darkness, blinked away grit. She coughed, tried to rise but couldn't. The air smelled of boiled flesh, as if God was making a stew of humanity. *Chloe!* she thought. White pain lanced her body, seared her soul.

Her eyes grew accustomed to the wan light. Rubble and a dirt-grey patina of dust blanketed everything. Chloe's photo lay in the dirt and she reached out and touched it with her fingers. A sob wracked her.

A scuffling noise brought her head around. She noticed a dark crack in the wall. She couldn't get her voice to work. *Help me,* Jane thought. *Please!*

Jane studied the far wall. A shadow spilled from the crack, moved forward then stopped, as if considering.

Her mouth moved weakly. *Help... daughter...* She wriggled feeble fingers.

The shadow shrunk, moved backwards, slipped through the crack.

Jane found her voice, but all she could do was cry.

Ezekiel blinks.

It is a world of ash and soot and broken stone. Burnt air sears his nostrils. A maddening hush descends. He shuffles forward, searching, stirring the dust and breathing it in. Ezekiel knows the dust is the crushed bones of this and all worlds, feeding an infernal global furnace. He is breathing in the dead, as he always had.

Half-heartedly, Ezekiel peers into the gloom. He remembers when memories were king, when memories were true. He knows that even if there were someone to speak with, he wouldn't share this memory.

Ezekiel slumps, turns back, wriggles through the crack and shuffles down the narrow passageway. Faintly, from the outer world, through the crack in the ceiling, comes the sound of sadness, as if all the angels of the world are weeping.

October Dreams

Her dreams were October dreams.

The girl was at that strange, carefree, happy age of dreaming and longing where one doesn't realize that they are unlikely to ever be that happy again. She dreamed of damp earth, crackling leaves, and wood smoke; warm spiced cider and cool winds; candied apples, and capering ghosts; grinning pumpkins and the boundless night.

The girl dreamed orange and black.

Then the girl grew older. She excelled in high school. And her dreams changed. They were filled with boyish grins, twining limbs, and soft smiles. She went to University. She found a job.

The world grew serious.

And still she dreamed, but she dreamed less, because now she wasn't a girl, but a woman, all grown up. And grown-ups, she knew, rarely dreamt. Grown-ups weren't expected to dream.

She fell in love and got married. And he wasn't the man of her dreams—who could be?—but he was good and kind and loved her. What dreams she still had she put on hold, and had a child, a girl, beautiful beyond words. She named her Autumn. And the woman who was once a girl was happy, yes, but it was a different happy. It wasn't the wild exuberance of infinite possibilities. It wasn't orange and black. It was contentment. And she was content to be content.

And life, as it does, passed.

The woman who was once a girl grew old. Her daughter Autumn dreamed too, but they were different dreams. Autumn found a good job, got married, moved away, and had children of her own. The woman's husband, who never knew of her dreams, grew infirm and passed away.

The woman who was once a girl wept quietly.

She grew older. She grew lonely.

She dreamed, again, of leering Jack-O-Lanterns, burning leaves, fresh-baked harvest pies, wet sidewalks, and pumpkin-scented winds. She dreamed of witches, demons, ghouls, and zombies.

She dreamed of darkest night.

She dreamed of the dead.

Time passed. The world quietened. The woman quietened. She

waited… waited, and dreamed her October dreams. She could smell the season, the slow rot. Still she waited. And finally there came a knock on the door, and she could hear them outside, chuckling, shuffling, rustling like orange leaves in a damp wind, tiny feet stomping, nervous and excited chatter.

The old woman who was once a young girl with dreams smiled, eased herself painfully from her chair, and moved to the door. She pulled some candy from a bowl, opened the door, wishing—*hoping*—for a trick, a child-like prank. She stood there, grinning. And all the children turned, scampered and skittered away, shrieking, as if they'd seen a ghost.

Or something worse.

Desert of Sharp Sorrows

Sorrows

with Jonathan William Hodges

There was Myra and there was the sun, descending.

The sun hung low on the horizon, a blood orange crushed, its pulp smearing the sky, leaving a yellow and purple band of light the color of her hidden welts. Her hidden shame.

When the last light leaked from the sky, the cold came and gripped her like a vise. Like Ian's vindictive hands.

Myra hadn't realized the desert would get so cold. She shivered, folded her arms, winced when her hand touched tender biceps. She probed the carefully concealed parts of her body, touching all the places Ian had handled. The pain registered from places much deeper than mere nerves.

No, she hadn't realized a lot of things.

Myra stood in a dirt rut before her cooling, ticking Toyota with its weak, wan headlights—sickly eyes spearing the gathering twilight. The wind whispered, then cut at her face: a rough lover. Ancient orange dust swirled across the plain, scratched her eyes. She trembled. It was so cold. But she was here, in the desert. Myra had always wanted to see the desert. Wanted to walk, alone, across the open expanse underneath a limitless sky. She thought, once, she might be able to walk here forever.

She'd never weighed the significance of forever.

Rocks and shrubs dotted the desert basin, a few small cacti; she thought it would be barren, a reflection of the cold landscape of her heart. In the dying light she could make out a crooked mesquite tree, a hearth for shadows.

She turned, left imprints in the landscape that would soon be lost, forgotten. She trudged to the car, slid into the seat, keyed the engine. The headlights winked, dimmed, then flared brightly, spotlighting the tree. A tinny song squawked from the A.M. radio: *still… haven't found… what I'm looking for.*

No, Myra thought, *I haven't*. She grimaced. She remembered the sun-glassed singer, the hit song. She owned the vinyl album: *The Joshua Tree*. Bought it in a used record store. She wished it were here with her now if only to look at the cover art. A reference point. Perhaps she could find a Joshua tree. *The* Joshua tree.

She remembered Ian, when he'd seen the picture on the back of the album, snorting derisively, claiming it blasphemous to use that image, to listen to that music, because the tree was named after the prophet Joshua from the Old Testament. How the tree mimicked Joshua's upraised arms as he beckoned his people to the promised land.

Myra grimaced. *Promised land.* She once thought the desert might be her own promised land. Now it was cold and without boundary, like space, like the ocean, like the places people went to become lost.

The song petered out and she turned off the radio. She steered the car down the pitted rut for several hundred yards before pulling off and parking under a mesquite tree. Night fell like a dark and heavy blanket, suffocating. Angry, sharp stars glittered in the night sky, cold, hard-edged. Outside the tiny car, the wind sang. And its song was high and keening, full of pain and torment and sorrow.

Myra reached around, yanked a sweater from a plastic bag on the back seat. She hunched down into her seat, snuggled under the sweater, and stared up at the star-studded sky. Her stomach rumbled, complained, and she glanced back at her few belongings packed into plastic grocery bags. No telling how long she'd need the food to last, so she ignored her body's pining. Her last meal had been in Lake Havasu. But she couldn't remember now if that had been earlier today or yesterday. She *did* remember the man beside her at the diner counter, though.

His eyes had been bright and angry like the desert stars. Skin like worn leather. His mouth gaunt and hungry, cheekbones wide and angular. A face of sharp sorrows.

Strange, she'd thought, the way a man could wear his life like that. The way a man, a woman, could become a portrait of that which they wished to hide the most. Her bruises showed the same as his anguish.

She'd had the feeling she'd seen this man elsewhere, that this wasn't their first encounter. He was a familiar stranger. She realized now it was his heart she knew. His pain.

He'd sat in silence while she browsed the menu. She had ordered coffee and a turkey sandwich. She'd blown on her coffee more than she drank it, watching the steam rise, hoping for it to spell out the way, to map uncharted territory, to, for once, make things clear. He had not read a paper, not talked to the waitress or other patrons. He simply sat and stared at his plate, the bread crumbs and smear of grape jelly like a stain of crusty blood. When the waitress had periodically cleared the counter of emptied plates, she'd always left his behind. Empty. Blank. Not like his expression.

He did not raise his head when he spoke to her the first time, as she'd picked up the second half of her sandwich. And that faint feeling of familiarity washed through her, his words spoken with a sense of knowledge and intimacy. As if they were secret lovers.

"There's not a thing in this life that don't happen for a reason," he'd told her. His accent had been unusual, and she'd found herself simultaneously enchanted and threatened.

"The good, the bad. Any of it. It's all got a purpose."

She'd offered him a polite smile, took a bite of her sandwich, and turned her head to look out the far window, away from him, as if he might vanish if ignored, as if ghosts didn't exist so long as no one believed in them.

"This ain't any different."

She'd laid down her sandwich, sipped at her coffee, bitter on her tongue.

"The way I see it, we're both here at this diner for a reason. Either I be needing you, or you be needing me."

Needing you. The words were still foreign to her.

The man had reached into a pocket and pushed something along the counter, left it beside her cooling porcelain mug.

"Here," he'd said, and raised his tanned hand to reveal a small, black leather pouch. "Take it."

She spoke to him for the first time. "What is it?"

"It'll help you find your way."

Myra had felt his stare. She'd glanced up, saw his bright, angry eyes; his hungry mouth. Younger than she first realized, hardly older than herself, he'd seemed to possess a wisdom she couldn't recognize. She wondered what it would feel like to kiss that hungry mouth. To once again feel greedy, passionate lips. And whether she could drink his knowledge like ambrosia from off his tongue. Instead, she'd turned away. "No thank you."

"Please," he'd said. "I've no use for it any longer."

She'd glanced again to the pouch, touched it. The fabric was soft but stiff. Like a small carcass. It emanated enchantment, as if magic lay within. Honest magic. If only she'd ever believed in such a thing. She'd taken the pouch from the countertop, stuffed it in the pocket of her loose-fitting jeans, took a deliberate sip of her cold coffee to settle her nerves, to quell this nervous energy.

"Happy?" she'd asked, heart pounding, embroiled now with a lurking edginess. She turned to find the space beside her empty but for a stark white plate stained with a blob of grape jelly. And long after he'd left she found herself wondering about his terse and hungry mouth, his sharp desert eyes.

Myra shook the memory from her head. Under the cool, bejeweled desert sky, with the strange man's voice ringing in her head and an unfamiliar contentment smoldering in her heart, Myra fell asleep.

She dreamed beneath a desert sky.

Myra woke cold and alone.

She blinked the sleep from her eyes, sat up from the modest recline of her front seat. Shivered. *Christ*, she thought, her arms coming up to cross and slip beneath her armpits, *who'd have thought the desert would be so cold?* She glanced at the rearview mirror, stared at her impassive face. The black beret she sported sat askew on her head and she lifted it, stared at the few clumps of wispy hair still clinging to her skull like strange sea anemones. She placed the beret back atop her head. She didn't care what she looked like. Not really. Not anymore. The small hat was protection from the scorching desert sun. At least that's what she told herself. She hoped she wasn't so vain, so shallow. Not at this point. There were more important things upon which to dwell.

A sharp pain stabbed her gut.

Myra tossed off the sweater and stepped from the Toyota. She walked around the mesquite tree, pulled down her pants, squatted and pissed. The stream of urine left a warm, steaming puddle. Seeing nothing with which to wipe herself, Myra straightened and pulled up her pants.

She turned, squinted into the horizon. The desert was still and cold and beautiful. A stark scene of serenity.

How many lives, she wondered, *quelled beneath this sand?*

Briefly Myra saw movement down in the basin, a shadowy form separating from a tree. She blinked. There was a man down there, standing stock still, staring her way. She thought of hulking Ian, stalking her. Yet deep in her heart, in that place that still held feelings and intuition, she knew it was *him*, the man from the diner.

Either I be needing you, or you be needing me.

But Myra didn't need anyone.

Myra didn't need anything.

She slid a hand under her shirt, touched the stark, bare spot near her heart where her breast had once been. She rubbed the bumpy landscape. Barren, like the desert. She didn't need the breast. She'd never had kids, and even if she had Myra didn't believe she'd have breast-fed. Her hand probed the rough-hewn skin. Another missing piece of her life. No, Myra didn't need anything.

Myra dug into her pockets, searching for her keys, and felt something foreign. She pulled out the small black pouch of worn leather. She'd forgotten about it, purposefully not inspected it the night before. She felt silly for taking it at all, mildly wary.

The leather was warm to the touch, and there was something hard inside, like a block of stone. Or, she thought grimly, a lump of metastasized flesh. She unzipped the pouch, pulled out a small, heart-shaped, silver box. The box had a small hasp, which she unclasped. She opened the hard silver heart. It was a compass with a bright yellow day-glo needle. Instead of the familiar compass points—N, S, W, and E—it bore words, a strange cursive script that wrapped around the compass dial: *Life, Love, Sorrow,* and *Death*. The needle hovered halfway between *Sorrow* and *Death*, edging down, ever down.

She grimaced, remembered the man's words. *It'll help you find your way.* Myra snapped the compass shut, placed it in the pouch, and returned it to her pocket. Another cruel joke. She fished her keys from her other pocket and returned to the car.

Myra didn't suspect she needed any help finding death. She'd hovered within its proximity her entire life.

She maneuvered the car along the pitted ground, down into the vast basin, until the track stopped and the ground became too rocky to traverse. She braked, turned off the engine, stepped from the car, and listened to the cooling engine tick down like a dying mechanical heart.

She lifted a hand above her eyes and squinted into the bright horizon. It was warming considerably, the taste of salt forming on her upper lip. In the distance, shimmering heat waves rippled, distorting the landscape, ghosts rising up. She thought she glimpsed a vague shape of a man, *that* man, the stranger from the diner, moving slowly across the rust-colored terrain.

Myra lifted her arm, waved. "Hey," she shouted. "Hello." Her voice was muffled, ineffectual, suffocated and lost in the vast desert. The figure stopped moving, and Myra couldn't be sure in the wavering heat if it really was a man after all. Perhaps it was a Joshua tree, she thought. She tried once again, cupping her hands at either side of her dry mouth.

"Hello!"

No answer. Of course not. No one ever had any answers for Myra. Not her doctors. Not her former friends. Not Ian. *Especially* not Ian. No answers. Only questions.

Her fingers brushed the soft welts on her upper arms that she wished weren't still there. She wished the pain would vanish as easily as the home, the friends, the man she'd left behind. Her hand flitted, bird-like, near the loose fabric of her blouse, lingering over the dead space, wishing there was something underneath.

She reached into the back seat and grabbed the plastic bag with her possessions. Turned and started to walk across the desert floor, toward the distant figure she wasn't sure was a figure at all.

Couldn't be sure of anything at all. The one constant in her life.

Nothing stayed the same for long.

Myra moved deliberately across the sand. Her sneakers trod on small, sharp stones that jabbed through the rubber soles and pricked her feet.

The morning grew hot, stifling; the desert ground gave off heat like a cooking griddle. Myra continued her journey, picking her way past rocks and shrubs. She reached into the bag, retrieved a bottle of water, and gulped it quickly down. The tepid water did little to slake the thirst building in her. There was a strange hunger as well. A hunger that craved more than only food.

As she moved across the desert basin she could still see the figure of the man in the distance. He wasn't any closer, but he didn't seem any further away either. Instead, as Myra walked, the distance remained the same, as if this were some strange carnival ride; the prize was always out of reach.

She remembered when she'd first found the lump. Myra wasn't one to normally perform self-examinations. But she'd woken that day and known something was amiss. She had sensed it—a strange quality to the air, to her surroundings, to her mood. Overnight the world seemed to change to a dreamy landscape wherein nothing was as it had been.

So, as she'd stepped from the shower, Myra moved to her dresser and sat naked before the mirror. Staring at her bland face, she wondered when a smile had last crossed her features. She forced one then, a strained smile, and her face twisted in a grim rictus. She'd sat hunched over, as if there was a heaviness on her shoulders, on her life. So she wasn't really surprised to find another heaviness, a hard mass, on the underside of her left breast. Myra, sitting naked and alone in her bedroom, had sighed and made a doctor's appointment.

One in every eight women in North America will develop breast cancer, Myra was told. One in eight. Bad odds.

Trapped in her house, Myra had taken to walking. She'd wake, and once Ian left for the day, would venture out the front door, pick a direction, and go. She soon discovered there was a world outside her door, outside her dirt-streaked windows. North, south, east, west. Love, life, sorrow, death. It didn't matter. She walked, slow and steady, taking in the sights, smells, and sounds of the city, of her neighborhood. In all her years in this part of town, she'd never really explored the area, never really *seen* it. People gardened, washed cars, played softball. They sat on porches and read, smoked cigarettes, sipped beers. Children played hopscotch and skipped double-dutch.

People were outside, living. It took Myra dying to discover that.

Then one day, in a dark part of the city that she'd never, in her earlier years, ventured to, she saw a poster in the window of a used record store and it stopped her dead in her tracks. *U2: The Joshua Tree.* Four young men standing in a barren desert, and behind them stood dark hills like angry, raised welts. Myra had stared at the poster, past the innocuous band members to the desert, to the hills rendered in black and white and shades of grey. A chiaroscuro. She walked into the store, found the album in a corner bin. She flipped the cover over, and there, on the back, was the tree, off to the right, solitary. The band members stood to the left, two in the distance, two in the foreground, the lead singer's head cropped out of the photo as if he weren't important. And he wasn't.

The tree was.

The lone tree struck a chord deep in Myra. It was crooked, bent, like a lot of people. It was also strong and proud. Two large branches spread out on either side, like open arms. Welcoming. She decided, then and there, she would go to the desert. She would go to the tree.

At the counter, paying for the album, the man at the register asked, "Do you have what you need?" And Myra had looked up, she now realized, into a face of sharp sorrows.

So here she was, in the desert, clutching a plastic grocery bag, wearing a black beret, staring at a distant image of a man or tree. Glad if it were either the tree or the man.

Another stride along the desert floor, then another. One foot after the other, toward… well, she didn't rightly know. It was enough that she was moving, never mind the goal. She was looking for something. *Isn't everyone*, she thought. For the first time in her life she was moving forward.

Myra walked. The sun followed her, moved across the sky, a beacon. The heat scorched her like a worm trapped on a sidewalk after a summer storm and left to bake on the hard concrete. The far figure stood impassive, a sentinel on the horizon. Her feet carried her over the stony earth, past small flowering shrubs and spiky plants of cacti. Little brown lizards darted in front of her, full of life. The desert wind sang low. And the figure, the man in the distance—for Myra was certain it was *him*—inched ever closer. Briefly, Myra had the impression of a large wooden cross, but it vanished, like dreams do, and she saw him, waiting with arms wide open. She smiled, hurried forward, stumbling over the rocky terrain. She marched across the sharp desert floor, plastic bag in one hand, the other hand holding the beret fast to her head. Orange sand blew in her face, stung her dry eyes. She blinked.

He was closer.

The sun set, leaving a red twilight the color of thin blood. Night eased slowly across the vast sky. But Myra still saw him. He was a dim silhouette, within shouting distance.

Myra called out "I have everything I need." She fished the small leather pouch from her pocket, opened it. Pulled out the silver heart-shaped box. She imagined the box pulsed, as if alive, like a real heart. She didn't need to open the compass to know where the needle pointed. Her life, it seemed, always wavered somewhere between sorrow and death.

As she drew nearer, night fell fast. Stars twinkled brightly, hotly, as if they held an incandescent rage. He fell, too, crumpling, folding in, laying down on the hard, barren ground.

Myra ran, her beret flying off, carried on the night wind. She reached him, breathless, and knelt at his side as the ground poked her legs. But it wasn't *him*. It was a tree. A Joshua tree. Myra wasn't surprised. And the tree, like Myra, was tired. So very tired. It didn't need anything anymore.

Holding tight to her heart-shaped box, Myra lay down in his arms. She imagined his hungry mouth. She turned, stared up at the angry stars.

She dreamed beneath a desert sky.

Blink

This story starts here, at this first line. First lines are important. The first draft began with this line:

"I thought you'd be taller," she says.

I blink. "Me too."

She laughs. A good start, I think. Every story needs a good beginning.

"And," I add, "I thought you'd look like your LoveMatch profile picture."

"Me too," she echoes, smiling. Then, smile fading, "That's some other me."

I pick up my beer glass, the cardboard coaster stuck to the bottom. "We all have some other version of ourselves," I say. "Other identities. Avatars. It's the new reality."

"Do you write science fiction?" she asks. "Your profile said you were a writer."

I grin, gulp beer. "Yes. That's one version of me."

"Oh," she says, disappointed.

"What?" I ask. "What is it?"

She sips her drink, some fruity concoction. "Nothing really," she says. "I don't read that stuff—science fiction. Never appealed to me." Her lips circle the straw, suck. "I thought we might talk about books. Writers."

I try a joke. "It could be worse. I could write horror."

She stares at me. Still good, I think. Characterization. Every story needs good characters.

We are quiet a while, sipping our drinks, glancing around the bar. Actually, scratch that. A bar is too cliché. I'll try to keep the clichés to a minimum. It isn't my strong suit.

Instead, we're at the... zoo. It's a brisk day. High grey sky knotted with thick dark clouds. A chill breeze. Damp and salty. Autumn, then. Near the sea.

We're at the ape house, watching one of the male primates masturbate.

I clear my throat. "We can, you know," I say. "If you like."

She blinks, puzzled.

"Talk about books," I say. "I'm not completely inept. I have read outside my genre." I cough. "On occasion."

She laughs, and I relax. It's a good sign. I thought we were heading for a rough patch, but the story is progressing.

After the ape house is the lion's den. The lions lie still, sleeping or dead. The clouds are thinning; the day brightening.

"What are you working on?" she asks.

"Hmmm," I say, distracted, staring at the dead lions.

"Your writing. What are you working on?"

I turn away from the dead animals. "Why don't we talk about you?"

"I... I," she starts, but just shrugs.

Of course, I haven't really constructed her yet. She's mostly me. A facsimile. Another avatar.

"Mabel," I say, and it's an old-fashioned name but she seems pleased with it. "I'm sorry, Mabel, but your profile was a bit sparse. You're a... paramedic?"

No reaction. She's as dead as the lions. "An actress?" I say, hopefully.

A weak smile. She says, "A writer."

I stare at her. Then I laugh. She grimaces. A lion yawns. Not dead, then.

"Sorry," I mutter. Too easy, I think. Too cliché, recreating myself. Lazy writing. Yes, write what you know. Still, it's lazy.

She's quiet, wide-eyed, looking around the zoo. She blinks, and something shifts, changes. It's like a television screen winking off.

Salt air and cool wind. Dark wet sand underfoot. We're at the... beach? Sky like an Etch-A-Sketch. Still autumn, then. All this scene-jumping isn't good. Revisions are needed.

"You didn't answer my question," Mabel says.

Further up the beach, in the shallow tide, there's a desk with a laptop open on it. There's a dark figure sitting at the desk, hunched over, typing. My eyes are wet. From the sea-wind.

"I... I, hmmm," is all I can muster.

She sighs, impatient, a tad angry. "Your writing." She's staring at the figure in the foamy surf, typing, as if addressing them, not me. "What are you working on?"

"Short stories," I answer. "My favourite form. Science fiction." I dry my eyes on a rough coat sleeve. "There's no money in it, though," I add quickly, defensively.

"Oh," she says, disappointment or regret tingeing her voice.

"What?" I ask. "What is it?"

She sips her drink, some fruity concoction. "Nothing," she says. "I just don't read that stuff."

It's as if we've already had this conversation. Where'd she get the drink? Was that a previous construct?

"I was thirsty," she says.

"Huh?"

She smiles, takes another sip. "The drink. I was thirsty."

It's quiet. Too quiet. The tide is soundless; the wind suddenly mute. My head hurts. We've reached the figure at the desk, bent to the keyboard, typing. There's nothing on the screen. It's white. Blank save for a large vertical black slash, a cursor, blinking like a judging eye. Then there's a choking, gasping sound and the dark figure slumps, falls into the dark tide and is carried out to sea. My eyes tear up. There's a pain in my chest. The world wavers, ripples, shifts again.

"What's happened?" I ask.

No answer. Mabel doesn't know. How could she?

But why don't *I* know?

Because you haven't thought it through.

Whose voice? A POV change! I blink. No, damn it, I'm not changing the point-of-view.

"No need," she says. "I will."

"You? You did that?"

Mabel smiles. "I didn't like him. Or you, for that matter. Not that there was any difference between the two."

He's trembling with rage. Another tilt, and there's a thrum in the air, like particles charging. His vision blackens, fades. He's shrinking, becoming less, or something else. "But you're only a character," he says. He blinks, curses her.

Blinking cursor.

She smiles. "Aren't we all?"

Mabel walks into the water, sits at the laptop and begins to type:

This story starts here, at this first line. First lines are important.

One thousand words later she stops and reads the story so far. Not satisfied, Mabel selects all the text and hits delete. She thinks she hears a tiny scream.

The screen is blank except for the infernal, blinking cursor, waiting.

Mabel doesn't know what to do.

She'll have to make something up.

Midnight Carousel

Young
nervous, impatient stallion
dark carnival dreams in his head, on his face
a queer leer, peering at the rusty, chained gate
the silent, shadowy midway.
He snorts
smoky streams from flared nostrils, stamps a foot
kicking sawdust, cranes his neck at the cold carousel.

Wind-whipped, wide-eyed memories swirl like dust
in a hot summer squall,
spinning, twirling,
a blur of noise and light, crush of warm bodies,
mad cackles floating on cotton candy air.

Sighing,
retreats, scampers back into place.
His grin a mad rictus, angry eyes wide,
glossy finish gleaming blackly midnight
atop the calm carousel.

Some Other You

The sky was dirty yellow and crumpled, like a sheet of glassine. It shifted and wavered. Todd studied it for some sort of sign, something that would give his life direction. A storm was coming, he knew.

That afternoon, on his bus ride home from work, Todd thought he saw Vivienne. He caught a glimpse of her walking past as the bus pulled up to a stop. She was with another man. They walked hand-in-hand along the cracked sidewalk, and the wound in Todd's heart opened afresh.

Todd scrambled off the bus and stood on the sidewalk, watching. When they began to leave his line of sight, Todd followed. He felt foolish, angry, and scared, but he continued to trail them, keeping well back so he wouldn't attract their attention. He studied the man. It was hard to discern from this distance, but he appeared to be about the same height and build as Todd, with similarly dark hair. Even his clothes looked like ones that Todd might wear. Todd wasn't surprised. Studies showed that most people who had affairs chose people who were eerily similar to their partners. Deep down they didn't want wholesale change, people mostly wanted something just slightly different but still familiar.

Vivienne and the man stopped in front of a cafe and had a brief conversation. She kissed the man on the cheek then went into the cafe alone. The man walked up the block a bit further then ducked into a pay phone. Todd grinned. Here was another of those strange creatures, like himself, who didn't have a mobile phone. He'd had one once, but it felt more like a ball and chain than a convenience. And he'd worried about radiation and cancer.

Todd averted his head, walked up close to the phone booth and considered an ancient playbill attached to wooden construction siding. *The Who* read the playbill. *Live! Maple Leaf Gardens. December 16. 1982.* Todd chuckled. The Who? Who, indeed.

Turning slightly, Todd could see the man in the phone booth in profile, bent in conversation, the phone cord trailing like a silver tentacle. Todd sidled closer to the booth. Just then, the man turned to Todd, moved the phone receiver from his face, and mouthed something through the glass. Todd gaped at the man and stumbled backwards, falling against the siding. He blinked, and a strange moan escaped his mouth. His head spun and he looked down to try to quell the spinning. When Todd gathered the courage to look back up at the phone booth, the man was gone. Trembling, Todd stood and braced himself against the old wood. He couldn't believe what he'd seen. Could he? Vivienne's 'other man' wasn't just similar to Todd in appearance, it *was* Todd. It had been himself in the booth, looking back out at some other version of himself. He tottered tentatively to the phone booth. As he leaned in to inspect the booth, he caught a momentary glimpse of himself reflected off the glass. That was it, he thought, somewhat relieved. It'd just been his reflection briefly superimposed on the other man's face, like a translucent mask. The thought gave him scant comfort.

There was a buzzing in Todd's head as storm clouds gathered in the darkening sky. He went in search of the subway to continue his way home. He wondered about Vivienne and when she might come home. He still held faint hope that she would return. Perhaps she was already there.

The phone rang in the dead of night. The incessant shrill ringing pulled Todd from a dream-plagued sleep. He rolled over sleepily and peered at the glowing green digits on the alarm clock. 4:11. If it were up to him, he wouldn't even have a phone. But Vivienne insisted. Whoever it was, they wouldn't give up. The phone rang and rang, a deadly thrum in his head.

Todd rolled out of bed and stumbled down the hall. The ringing was loud in the tiny apartment, like an alarm bell. He was sure it would wake the neighbours. It reverberated around his head, and the apartment. Emptier now that Vivienne was gone.

He thought that they would be together forever, he and Vivienne. Thought that they'd build a life out of hopes and dreams and love. Love conquered all, didn't it? It didn't, he learned. People can fall out of love just as easily as they can fall in love. It was a harsh lesson, and his already fragile heart cracked a little further each time he thought about it. Which was often.

For a brief moment Todd considered that the caller might actually be Vivienne. But that was impossible, he knew. Still, when he lifted the phone's receiver it was with a sense of anticipation.

"Hello," Todd said. The phone cord seemed to squirm.

There was a hiss of white noise, a crackle of black static.

"Hello?" Todd repeated.

Then from the other end of the line came a soft chuckle and a familiar voice. "Hello," said the voice. And Todd shivered. The voice on the other end was Todd's own voice, or at least what Todd thought his voice sounded like in his head. He was almost certain of it. A click and the connection was cut, leaving dead air.

Todd placed the handset back in its cradle and stumbled to the kitchen table. The bottle of tequila was still there, still open. He grabbed the bottle by the neck, tilted it to his dry mouth and took a gulp of the fiery liquid. There had to be a reasonable explanation for it. He wondered if you could somehow phone yourself? He'd been having nightmares lately, mostly about Vivienne, and perhaps he'd imagined or dreamed the phone ringing and sleepwalked to it and his fumbling fingers made a strange connection, dialling himself. It was possible, wasn't it? Phone lines had always been a mystery to him. He distrusted them. All those voices travelling through air, getting in his head. How was it possible? Could you mistakenly call yourself? Then a sobering thought struck him. You *could* call yourself — if there was some other you.

When he woke, sometime past noon, there was a grey pallor to the sky and dark clouds spread across the horizon. In the bathroom, Todd looked at himself in the dull mirror. His own pallor was as grey as the outside world, and the face looking back at him seemed slightly different somehow, softer, as if his head had been a ball of putty clumsily reshaped by a disinterested child. But he didn't want to think about children. He half expected when he turned away from the mirror that his face wouldn't follow, that it would keep staring out from the dull patina, all soft and grey and time-worn. Unblinking. Todd moved slowly to the doorway and peered at the mirror from an angle. It appeared to be empty. Of course it was. What did he expect? Yet, when he walked into the next room he couldn't quite shake the feeling that he was being watched.

He'd missed work. Hadn't even called in sick. The thought of picking up the phone and calling in to report his absence filled him with a queer dread. Whose voice would he hear on the other end? Instead, he grabbed a large glass of orange juice and plopped down on the sofa in front of the massive plasma-screen television that he had purchased so that he could watch his reality television shows. An impulse buy that had angered Vivienne. "That reality isn't real, Todd," she'd said. What is real? he mused. Todd stared at the monstrosity. It was far too big for the apartment, as Vivienne had noted on a number of occasions. Its blank screen reflected blackly back at him. Todd could see himself—at least a vague shapeless version of himself—in the dark screen. The shape in the screen disturbed him. Something about its lumpishness made him queasy. He picked up the remote and powered the television on. Static filled the screen with a crackling thrum, like a billion excited stars in a churning night sky. He flicked through the channels and was met with the same flickering static on each. The cable was out again. The cable company was about as reliable as the telephone company. Not surprising, Todd thought, seeing as they were one and the same. Soon, if it already hasn't happened, one company will run everything. Still, Todd decided to leave the blue static on. It seemed a decidedly better choice to him than the blank, dark screen and the misshapen humanoid form he'd seen reflected back at him.

Todd glanced toward the window. The dark clouds had encroached closer, seemingly just outside the building, large and black and shot through with veins of lightning. They hovered, expectant, as if waiting. Then it began to snow and it seemed to mimic the static that had hissed from his plasma screen, as if, Todd thought, the whole canvas of the sky was nothing more than a large television or window onto the world, where we could passively and numbly watch events unfold, uninvolved and mostly uninterested.

He wondered about windows, mirrors, and blank television screens. He thought they were like portals to some other possible world, thin membranes that separated both worlds. And what would he find on the other side? Something terrible and alien? Or another world like this one, with another version of himself. Perhaps, he mused, there was another Vivienne out there, one that wouldn't betray him. Vivienne 2.0. An upgrade.

The subway was like a coffin. It was hot and cloying and smelled of sweat, tar, and spoiled meat. Todd was packed tight into the car, gripping a greasy pole as passengers bumped and jostled him. Everyone wore grey. Grey suits, grey skirts, and grey expressions. Todd stared at the subway car's window as the train shuttled and clacked along the ancient tracks. He saw his reflection wink in and out as the car moved from station to tunnel, from light to dark. His face seemed to change. He wondered if he'd be the same person at journey's end.

Todd's office was in the Port Lands, an area of the city that had seen better days, perched on the eastern outskirts of the downtown core. From the subway he had to take a bus. There were few passengers on the antiquated bus, but it smelled much like the subway had, as if mass transit in urban areas was required to smell of piss and sweat. As the bus bounced along the pot-holed streets, Todd stared out the window. Everything appeared blurred and out of focus, as if a thick grease had been liberally applied to the bus's windows, rendering the scene in a grimmer pre-Raphaelite fashion. The snow continued to fall, more like grey ash now than proper snow. The bus trundled past abandoned factories, their smoke stacks stained a matte-black or rusted to a vibrant orange-brown. Bricks crumbled and fell from buildings. Glass windows had been smashed and covered haphazardly by boards nailed in an X pattern over the windows. On the sidewalks could be seen shivering lumps of humanity, dressed in filthy rags. Like an invasive species, graffiti adorned much of the exteriors of the abandoned buildings. On the side of one building, in large block letters, Todd read R.U.U? Past new buildings, in the port proper, ships and cranes listed in the heavy, brackish water. Occasionally, Todd would notice a ripple or tremor on the water's surface and he wondered what stirred beneath it.

Todd exited the bus and stood in front of his grey, flat office building. He suspected his employers were too cheap to rent proper office space downtown. Inside, the office was as flat and grey as the exterior. Todd managed to get to his desk without having to confront a colleague. A small mercy, to be sure. At his desk, the red light on his phone was flashing. There were messages awaiting him. He stared at the blinking red light uneasily and sat down. There was a yellow sticky note affixed to his computer monitor, on which was printed *Who are you?* Todd grimaced, blinked, stared at the yellow square. *Where* are you? it read. Not *Who*.

There was a shuffling behind him. Todd turned to find Carruthers standing at his door, clutching a sheaf of papers.

"Ah, Simmons," Carruthers said, "how very thoughtful of you to join us. You're a difficult man to track down." Carruthers nodded toward Todd's desk. "Don't you ever answer your phone?" he asked.

Todd blanched. Was it possible he'd missed an entire workday and they hadn't even taken notice?

"I've... been busy," Todd said.

Carruthers snorted. "Well, yes, of course. If you weren't busy, we'd have no need for you. Would we? We'd find a better you."

For a brief moment Todd imagined Carruthers' face changing. It rippled, went grey, and filled with a starry static. Then it rippled again and returned to its doughy normalcy.

Todd rolled backwards a few inches in his chair, pressing himself against his desk. "A better me?" Todd croaked.

Carruthers stepped forward, dropped the bundle of papers on Todd's desk. "It's month's end, Simmons. Get these reports into the books by end of day." Todd looked at the stack of reports and glanced back up, but Carruthers had already gone. He reached over and plucked the sticky note from his monitor, crumpled it and dropped it into his recycling bin. Then he peered around his cheerless, windowless office, at his cluttered desk, his grimy walls and the worn, faded carpet. He wished he had a window. He wondered if it was still snowing.

The morning drifted by in a haze of spreadsheets, numbers, and data. He didn't stare too long at his computer monitor, too afraid to see what the reflection might reveal. His phone rang several times but he didn't answer it. The blinking red light taunted him. When his stomach complained, he grabbed his jacket, his bagged lunch, and left the building. He strolled down to the docks to eat in peace.

The dirty grey snow fell like dead ash. Todd looked up at the wide, carnivorous sky. Dark clouds continued to trace their way across the fabric of this world, slow, deliberate, like misshapen zeppelins. Beyond the black formations, a pewter sky stirred, brewing darkness and trouble. It seemed to hover over Todd, within arm's reach. He felt as though he could stand up and touch the sky, pull it apart, and climb through its pearly opalescence to that other, better side. Perhaps he'd find his other self on the other side.

It was Vivienne who'd first put the idea into his head that there might be another Todd. She'd sat down beside him on the sofa, muted the television. Todd stared at her. Her hands twisted in her lap, and a small smile played across her face. He'd glanced back at the silent television. "I'm pregnant, Todd. We're going to have a baby." She reached out, grabbed his hand. He'd turned back to her, numb, and as silent as the television that flickered in his periphery. "A little Vivienne or Todd of our own," she'd said. Instead of a miniature version of himself, Todd pictured a grown-up version. A version that resembled him slightly, but wasn't really him. A different version or entity that was fucking his wife. And in his mind's eye she enjoyed it more. The smile fell from her face and she said, "Are you okay, Todd? What is it? You don't seem yourself." So he'd blurted, "Is it mine?"

Then she was gone.

A screech from a gull pulled Todd from his reverie. He'd been scared, is all. Nervous. The thought of another him had filled him with a quiet terror. Now it excited him. He now knew that there was another him out there.

Todd looked at the dark, swirling sky, at the black, wavy water; those thin places where he thought he might be able to cross over and find his true self. He opened his bagged lunch, pulled out an apple, and bit into it. It was bitter.

Later, on the bus ride home, he noticed the same garish graffiti on the side of a building. R.U.U?

Are you you?

It was very late when Todd got home. He couldn't remember where he'd been or what he'd done. The apartment smelled strange, like electricity and meat, and his telephone was ringing. It rang and rang, persistent. He walked over and yanked the phone cord from the wall. Still, it seemed the phone rang, as if it had always been ringing.

Todd walked past the television, glanced at the blank screen. He moved past the window, stared at the soot-grimed panes. He shuffled into the bathroom and looked into the mirror. Each reflective surface, each thin place, showed him the same shadowy, wispy countenance, the same haggard wraith, as if Todd were merely a ghost of his former self. He was tired. So fucking tired. Todd shambled into the bedroom.

He stood in the small dark room and stared at the bed. The smell was worse in here. There was someone or some *thing* under the covers, unmoving. He tottered over to the bedside and stared down at the covered figure. He placed a hand on the rumpled sheet. The figure was still and cold. Todd placed both hands on the edge of the cover, ready to pull the sheet away, but hesitated, uncertain, doubt clouding his mind. He thought, hoped, it might be himself under the cover, some other version of him, but he stood there trembling, gripping the sheet, too afraid to pull it away in case it wasn't.

Hark at the Wind

Amanda. His beloved of the sky.

This high up, the wind is a banshee. He is on the balcony, squinting into the sallow day. The sky is green and rumpled. Soon it will be nightfall and he will have to go inside. *They* can climb, he knows. He hears them—pictures them moving crab-like up the brickwork.

Down. Look down.

He has not looked down in a very long time. Not since that morning. He is afraid of what he might still see.

The wind has a voice. Amanda thought it was the voice of angels, beckoning. He thought it was the senseless shrieking of a world gone mad. He'd been right. But it didn't matter. Death calls in different voices.

Finally, he looks down at the forlorn street, the cracked and blackened sidewalk. Empty.Like an abandoned childhood play-set.

He blinks into the greyness, dry-eyed.

He'd woken that day to a pallid sky and a chill breeze blowing into the apartment through the open balcony door. She'd reached for the sky, but had fallen short. He'd looked down at her ragged form. At dusk she stirred, cradled her ropy innards, and crawled away. Squinting, he saw a dark smear.

Later, he'd moved to the top floor.

In the apartment he found a pair of binoculars. He scopes the high-rise across the way. It's been weeks since he's seen anything. He might be the last of his kind. He looks beyond the building, to the stand of thin maples. Past the trees are the bay, and the marina. He's pondered trying to make it to the marina. The open water held vast appeal. But the distance is further than it looks, he knows, and he wouldn't make it before nightfall.

He smells damp wood-smoke.They are waking. He drops the binoculars and gazes up. A sky like wet ashes, now. Sky and trees. The sky scorned as timber. The trees beloved of the sky. He wishes the world were all sky and trees.

He steps into the apartment. Pulls the jury-rigged metal gate closed. Locks it.

The cat rubs against his leg. He strokes its spiky orange fur. It purrs, swishes away and hops onto the sofa. The cat makes a show of grooming itself, then nestles into a cushion. He smiles, imagining himself a cat. He doesn't know the cat's name. Doesn't want to know. It's easier, he thinks, if you don't give a name to something or someone. Easier not knowing. He sits beside the cat, leans back, closes his eyes...

...and wakes to faint noise, a scratching. Something is in the hallway, clawing at his door. The cat is hissing. And another noise, from outside; the shrill wind calling. Beyond that sound, another. A scuttling. As if something he once loved were steadily crawling up the building, to slip over the railing onto the balcony, to stand and grin blackly, and shriek and shriek, beckoning, night after night, like the infernal wind.

Other Summers

with Ray Cluley

The moon is fat and bright, holding back the dark. A warm wind blows across the high summer grass, touching their faces, their sticky summer skin, and moves on, its faint summer song trailing and fading like summer itself. Dying.

The girls giggle, nervous, excited; their faces glow in the shine of the moon, wide and innocent still. The boys shuffle, kick at the dusty ground, snort, push and shove and laugh.

"Summer," Mary-Ann says.

"Summer," Alisha repeats, wistful.

"There'll be others," Ryan says.

"Other summers," Josh agrees.

The high grass sways. They wait, giggling and sniggering. "Shush," one of them says, and that gets them laughing.

Sixteen years old, all of them. Their skin smooth, eyes bright like glass marbles, hair thick and glossy, lips red as cherry popsicles. The four of them stand in the tall honey-grass, looking out beyond the field and the fat moon's brilliance to the edge of darkness. Waiting.

"When?" Mary-Ann asks.

"When?" Alisha repeats, anxious.

"Soon," Ryan says, staring into the dark.

"Real soon," Josh agrees, licking his lips.

They are thin and bronzed, fidgeting, touching, all angles and questions. How? Why? Who? When?

Then, from the inky darkness, a sound, faint and growing. Music. An organ, an accordion, like a child's wind-up toy. And as they watch, their thin bodies aquiver, coloured lights wink on, lighting the darkness in reds and blues, greens and yellows, like strands of Christmas lights strung across the night sky. Christmas in summer.

The warm wind carries the music, bright and cheerful, and brings the smell of popcorn and cotton candy, hot dogs and sweet corn, cola and sawdust and summer.

They smile their bright popsicle smiles.

"Now," Mary-Ann says.

"Now," Alisha repeats.

"Let's go," Ryan says.

"Yes, let's go now," Josh agrees.

Smiling, they move through the late-season grass that tickles the backs of their knees. Then down a dirt road, the contented moon at their backs smiling a benediction, toward the music and the lights to a gated entrance. But a simple chain fence isn't going to keep them out, not on this night, and they slip through easily to the other side.

They tremble with excitement, huddle close, brush against each other, skin on skin, hot breath mingling in whispers and more summer laughter.

"Here we are," Mary-Ann says.

"Again," Alisha says.

"It never changes," Ryan says.

"Some things don't," Josh says.

The music swells, fills the summer night with its melody, beckoning, pulling them toward it. A calliope, summer's sweet instrument.

They glide down the centre of the midway, past the Ring Toss, imagining the red hoops clacking off the milk bottles, a sound like summer rain against a window. They pass the cotton candy machine and its sweet pinkness, and the 'Test Your Strength' booth. Ryan flexes his muscles, grins. Over there is the Mirror Maze and the House of Horrors. They walk past the sweet corn and the hot dogs spinning on their warming plates, past booths with stuffed animals and games of chance. They move past the Tunnel of Love, and Josh holds Alisha's hand. Ryan wraps an arm around Mary-Ann, pulls her close.

"The best night of my life," Mary-Ann says.

"The absolute best," Alisha repeats.

"The four of us together," Ryan says.

"Yes, together," Josh agrees. "Always."

They huddle close, the four of them, shuffle as one through the saw-dusty grounds, past canvas-flapped tents boasting bearded women, centipede men, and cabinets of countless curiosities. They imagine the barker with his megaphone, beckoning, "Come one, come all, to the fantastic Freakshow! The greatest show on earth!"

Still the calliope plays. Light and then dark, soft and then swelling, carried on the night breeze: the music of laughter and dark mystery; of carnivals and funerals; of life and death; of summer itself. Endless summer.

The sweet summer wind gusts, swirls past them, prickling their skin with gooseflesh, tickling their noses with carnival scents; French fries and ketchup, burgers and coke, peanuts, popcorn, and liquorice. It carries mystery and regret, sorrow and happiness, and all the hopes and dreams of children everywhere. Or so it seems to them, this night, at this moment.

Then, there it is, in front of them: the Merry-Go-Round. Quiet and still, though the music plays on, the lacquered horses are wide-eyed and open-mouthed, frozen, hooves raised, manes flowing.

The four of them, suddenly silent, step onto the platform and each climbs a horse. For a moment, their faces resemble those of the horses—stricken with fear. Then, slowly, the Merry-Go-Round stutters forward and they hoot and grin.

"Hurry!" says Mary-Ann, excited fit-to-burst now that the long ride has begun. She rocks back and forth on her horse, eager for more speed.

"Come on, let's go!" Alisha says, urging her horse. She clutches at its neck and leans low, hair caught in the breeze of their new movement.

"We're off!" Ryan announces. He holds both arms high, grips the bright horse with his thighs, and turns in the saddle to look behind.

"It's begun!" says Josh. He holds his arms up like Ryan and increases the challenge by standing up in the stirrups.

Round and round they go, merrily, their wooden steeds rising and falling with the music.

"Faster!" Mary-Ann calls.

"Faster!" Alisha yells.

"Onward!" Ryan shouts.

"Yes, onward!" Josh cries.

The carousel rolls its calliope sounds in toots and whistles, melodies overlapping melodies to create an eternal chorus of rising, falling joy as bright as the stars, as bright as comets.

Mary-Ann looks at Ryan, pumping his arms and cheering. She

will kiss him tonight. She has decided it lots of times. One day, she knows, he will take her to Lake Point in the truck he bought from working all summer at the gas station and she will kiss him then, too. He will be on the college football team and she will be a cheerleader and they will kiss in his truck under a full moon.

Mary-Ann cheers, "It's wonderful!"

Alisha whispers into the ears of her horse, urges it on. It seems to hear her, to understand, because round and round they spin, faster and faster. The warm wind of dry summer tousles her hair, carries the aroma of other summers, summers gone and summers soon to be. Summers of cut grass and fresh drinks and fireworks. She hears them soar and burst and sparkle and their light shines back from the bright colours of their horses, the golden poles, the pipes of the glorious organ that sounds its giddy anthem of summer. One day she will watch them whoosh, flash, fall, and she will be with someone who loves her and holds her and drapes his jacket over her shoulders and tells her things that make her smile and laugh and *ooh* and *ahh*.

Alisha says, "It's perfect!"

Ryan hurries after the horses in front, fists in the air, never catching them but happy to chase, weaving up and down and around, around. He hears the calls of his friends, the cheers, and a new crowd of onlookers blurs as he passes them, and passes them again, and he knows that this is what a winning touchdown run feels like. He will slam the ball down to the ground and jump and others will catch him, lift him, parade him around and around as he punches his fists to the air with the same triumph he feels now.

Ryan exults, "It's ours!"

Josh closes his eyes and grins as the carnival din washes over him, takes him, lifts him, lowers him. He rushes forward forever, knowing that one day he will catch Alisha and maybe take her to the prom. Yes, he will take her to the prom and buy her a corsage and she will wear it and look beautiful and he will look smart and they will dance together. They will move close to each other. Afterwards they will watch the fireworks. The sky will be sunshine-bright, alive with colours. He will tell her the poems he is too afraid to write and she will lean in close because she likes them.

Josh says, "Yes, it's wonderful! It's perfect!"

Horses grin and snarl and gallop and fall; they run away from what is, run towards what will be. Faster. Louder. Faster.

"Give us more."

"Yes, give us more."

"Again, again."

"Forever."

Mary-Ann leans forward, cranes her neck, takes in the swirling lights, the swirling music, the swirling smells. She is giddy with it all. She grins, glances again at Ryan. Yes, she will kiss him, place her lips on his. They will be soft and wet and tender. With their chests pressed together her heart will thump against his. The summer wind will sing a love song, caress their flawless bronzed skin, prickle it in gooseflesh. Ryan will wrap a protective, warming arm around her and pull her closer. And even though she prides herself on the fact that she doesn't need this boy, this man-to-be, to protect her or to keep her safe, she concedes that it would feel good to be wanted, to be loved. Yes, she thinks, yes. Maybe this time.

In front of her, two bright lights appear in the dark. Twin moons, growing.

Alisha leans forward, wraps her legs tight around the lacquered horse. She trembles, wonders what it would be like to wrap her legs around a man one day, maybe even Josh. The thought sends a tingle through her and she rubs herself against the hard sculpted surface of the saddle. She gasps, holds on tight and rocks with the speeding horse. The wind whips her hair. She stares at Josh. She will marry one day, perhaps even Josh, perhaps not. She'll be a modern woman. There are plenty of jobs. She'll meet someone, marry him, and they will travel the world together. At night, in their hotel room, she will wrap her legs around him and buck against him. At least that's what she thinks this year. Maybe this time it will happen. Please, she thinks, please. And she holds on tight, bucks against the horse, closes her eyes when the bright lights appear ahead, spearing the night. She thrashes and moans against the horse, against the lights. She catches the sharp smell of something new in the night, like hot tar and gasoline, anxiety and fear, and when she opens her eyes again they're as wide as her horse's.

"Yes," Ryan repeats, but less enthusiastically this time, "it's ours." The Merry-Go-Round spins. In his head, images spin like those in a motion picture reel. He will score that winning touchdown and hear the adulation of the crowd. He will go to college, get his banking or drafting degree. He will become a banker, or an architect, and he will marry and have children, a handsome boy and a sweet girl. Maybe he will marry Mary-Ann. Sometimes he sees Mary-Ann alone, and sometimes they marry, and sometimes they don't have children: summers are full of infinite possibilities. But *this* summer, *this* time, he sees his children. He reads to his daughter at night. He teaches his son to ice-skate. He kisses their cheeks, hugs them close, and tries not to cry each night as he stands in their doorway and just watches them, these precious gifts, sleeping soundly.

A car horn blared. Tires screeched. He smelled scorched rubber. He keened forward, stared, and was momentarily blinded by lights careening across his vision. He reached across the passenger seat, the carousel boards, feeling for Mary-Ann.

Josh will be a writer. Other summers he is other things. He will sell a few poems for little money, then he'll sell some short stories to literary journals, and then he'll write a novel about love and death and hate and grief, endless summer, a novel that will be well-received but sell very few copies, a novel that he knows is good and that he is proud to have written. And he will meet someone, a man this time, and they will become close and will share their lives together, but Josh will secretly weep for their secret life because they live in the age of shame. Oh, these endless summers, Josh thinks. Some sad, some happy.

A cry made him look up. A fierce light in the night blinded him. Then came the squeal of tires, the terrible shrieking crash, and the smell of burnt rubber and gasoline and smoke. Alisha, he thought. Alisha.

Alisha couldn't breathe. She thought it was because she'd screamed it all out, but when she tried to inhale she only got smoke and heat and something sharp, something coppery. She knew these smells, knew all of them, knew them as well as she knew the candyfloss, the cola, the buttered pop-pop-popcorn, but those smells were gone now. The popping was not corn, she didn't know what it was but it wasn't popcorn and it wasn't good. She was dizzy, too, spinning around and around and around without moving. She didn't want to move. It hurt. "Mary-Ann, it hurts."

Mary-Ann held on tight. There was a funny taste in her mouth and her lips were red but not Popsicle, not toffee apple. Red and slick. There was a loud sound in her head like horses screaming but there were no horses. Then it was quiet and they were flying, fast, faster, round and round, but not the same way as before; up and round and round and down and round and round some more. They yelled together, friends in fear, crying a shared terror as they spun. Mary-Ann tried to call out for Ryan, where was Ryan, "Ryan?" and "Ryan!" but the only answer she got was a pain hard in the chest that thinned her breath to nothing.

Ryan fell, dropped, tumbled, and somehow he was outside when he used to be inside but he wasn't sure where, only that he was not where he was meant to be. None of this was how it was meant to be: it was always this way. He heard someone scream and it sounded like Alisha, heard his name and it sounded like Mary-Ann. He couldn't answer. The grass was under him, night-cool, dark and wet. What happened, Josh? Why? Why does it always happen?

Josh shielded his eyes but not from the lights; they were gone now. All of them. He didn't want to see. He no longer rose and he no longer fell. Nothing turned. The music had stopped and the rest was silence until the fiery light of a bright false dawn came with a whoomph and whoosh of heat more intense than any summer.

"No more," he says.

Alisha rests her face against the brass, caresses a painted mane, and looks to Mary-Ann.

Mary-Ann holds her piebald horse, reluctant to dismount, and looks back at Ryan.

Ryan lowers his arms. He nudges Josh.

Josh opens his eyes.

The moon was fat and bright, holding back the dark. A warm wind blew across the high summer grass, touched their faces, their sticky summer skin, and moved on, its faint summer song trailing and fading like summer itself.

Mary-Ann blinked, her eyes sticky with blood. She reached out, clutched at Ryan's ruined hands. "Your car is wrecked," she said, pulling a clot of hair and scalp from her face.

Ryan nodded, looked across the road at the couple staring at a truck that had flipped over. "Sorry about your truck," he said.

"My dad's truck," said the boy. His name was Josh. "He's going to be pissed."

The girl, Alisha, reached up to Josh's face, smoothed a flap of loose skin back into place. "Your dad will forgive you," she said. "I'm sure." She paused, and her body shook. "We were going to the fair."

Mary-Ann smiled weakly. She squeezed Ryan's hand. "So were we. It's a summer tradition."

Ryan said, "It isn't far, maybe we could all still go." He coughed wetly, spat something out he shouldn't have. "I love the Merry-Go-Round."

Josh grinned. "Yes. It would've been good."

"The best night of our lives," Mary-Ann whispered.

"The absolute best," Alisha repeated.

"The four of us together," Ryan said.

"Yes, together," Josh agreed. "Always."

The four of them move out into the field and stand in the tall honey-grass, looking out beyond the grassland and the fat moon's brilliance to the edge of darkness. Then, from the inky night, a sound, faint and growing. Music. A calliope. As they watch, coloured lights winked on.

Mary-Ann blinks, rubs blood from her eyes. Her hands pass through like wind through fog and she shrugs, smiles weakly. "Summer," she says.

Alisha coughs. She stares ahead. The carnival lights blur, wink in and out. A piece of gleaming red bone protrudes from her chest. She pushes it back inside, and then she can see through her hand to the ground below. "Oh, summer," she says.

Ryan sighs, pushes wet hair from his face. The girls are ahead of him, wavering like smoke. "There'll be other summers," he says.

Josh's face is wet with blood and tears. He trembles, tries to bite his missing lower lip. "Yes," he says, on the crest of weeping. "Other endless summers."

The summer song swells. Soon, they know, the music will once again fade and vanish, like summer itself.

Always dying.

Together they move through the tall late-season grass toward a world of infinite possibilities and endless summer.

Another Knife-Grey Day

Albatross screech

Churning knife-grey sea, charcoal-smudged sky, barren sand-tar
beach
sixty-five miles from nowhere
from anywhere

Typical knife-grey day

You, my captive albatross, atop a moss-brick sea wall, a pale
porcelain ovoid, lips smeared ruby red (sour cherry jam on a moon-
white breakfast plate)
eyes like bad pennies
a bat-wing coat flapping in the salty sea breeze
a blur of black vellum

You turn, afford a small sharp-toothed grin, a flicker of forked
tongue

Sly to your very end

In the sullen haze I pull the stake (as wooden and true as our love)
from the folds of my kelp-stiff cloak

Your penny eyes flash, your mouth opens gull-like, shrieks

Grinning, arms wide, you leap
I watch you fall into the mad sea, sink into the frothy crimson tide
Sixty-five miles from Portsmouth, from anywhere, from nowhere

I shuffle off into another knife-grey day

But the shrieking never ends

Absolution

Night. Harvest moon, fat and orange. The autumn wind sings songs of innocence and despair.

The girl is up in her room, gazing out the window. There are tears in her eyes, streaking her face.

There was a boy once. Louis. But he's gone. She hopes he comes back. Wishes for it, in fact, for the girl is lonely. She has no friends. She isn't like the other girls.

She wipes her eyes, dries her face.

She is smart, the girl. She reads books and magazines, even newspapers. Her teachers call her 'bright,' 'studious,' and 'assiduous.' She does not have to look up the word 'assiduous.' Her father calls her 'bookish,' and she fancies that.

She loves her parents the way all children do—grudgingly. And she loved Louis, too, she suspects, or she wouldn't be lonely, would she? Books aren't always enough, she thinks. She prays Louis will come back. After all, the dog came back. He isn't the same, the dog. He's smelly, mangy, and wary. But he's back. She remembers faint scratching at the door; a soft, sad mewling. When she opened the door, the dog growled. It was covered in mud and had a nasty head wound. The dog shuffled past her, leaving a trail of black dirt. *Poor thing*, she thought.

Louis, though, has been gone longer than the dog. She is worried. And lonely.

The girl tries to make friends, girls or boys, but everyone steers clear of her. Like the dog now, they hide whenever she approaches. Mostly, she stays in her room, studying.

For a time, the girl tried pets; hamsters & guinea pigs. Turtles. But they never lasted. And once they were gone, they never came back. They had tiny brains and tiny hearts. The girl, though, had a big heart. Big enough for love. Big enough for forgiveness. She thought the dog would be a better choice. Now the dog hates her. Everyone hates her. The girl hopes that when Louis comes back, he doesn't hate her. *If* he comes back.

So the lonely girl waits. She reads and studies, and thinks about Louis.

Louis was in her geography class. He sat in front of her. The girl would stare at his shiny chestnut-brown hair; at his small and perfect ears; his pale slender neck. Her heart would flutter madly, as if it were a caged thing seeking escape. Her body would tremble. Each day she would sit and stare, hoping he'd turn so she could see his eyes, his nose, his mouth. His mouth. She would doodle in her book—love poems; cupid hearts.

Then, one day, Louis turned, looked at her quizzically, then smiled. He was in full blush: pink face, red lips, and eyes shining. A quiver of nervous excitement shot through the girl. Like an electrical charge; something come to life. He passed a folded note to her. Something stirred in the girl, bloomed, opened up. She felt lighter. The world vibrated. Louis walked her home, carried her book bag. They didn't speak. Just smiled and stole side-long glances at each other.

That night, the girl's heart swelled. Her head spun. She dreamed of soft skin, bright eyes, and warm mouths.

The following day, in class, the girl couldn't get Louis' attention. Later, in the hallway, she saw him talking with another girl.

And the next day, Louis was gone.

So the girl stays in her room and studies her moldy books. She thinks about Louis. She knows she can forgive him. Hers is a heart big enough for absolution.

The girl looks up at the moon. It is big, bright, and full. Like her heart. The wind murmurs a strange lament.

Tonight, she thinks. Tonight, under the harvest moon, Louis will return. She looks at the book; at the runes chalked on the floor. She's done everything she can. She thinks it'll be just like the dog's return: There'll be a faint scratching, and a soft, sad mewling. Then she'll open the door and he'll growl at her. He'll be covered in mud. And he'll be sporting a nasty head wound.

She hopes he can forgive her.

All the Things
We Never See

Y ou can lose yourself, Susanna thought, become a ghost.

Susanna blinked, stared through the bus window at the ghosts on the street.

Dark-blurred figures, wet and frayed, their shadowy faces gaunt and pale, congregated on dirty street corners and followed the track of the bus as it lumbered through the city streets. Susanna studied them through the hazy window. They were watching her. She knew it. She watched them watching her. She was looking for Kevin, who'd lost himself and become a ghost—or something else entirely. Susanna didn't know what *they* were looking for. She shivered.

Kevin.

Presumed dead. That's what the authorities suspected. They wouldn't come right out and tell Susanna that Kevin was obviously dead, but after four months missing he'd either abandoned his life here for another in some exotic locale like the Grand Caymans, or, as was more likely, he'd fallen into a canal somewhere.

Susanna knew better. *They* had gotten him. She only had a very vague notion of who *they* were, but Kevin knew. And he'd paid for his knowledge.

The weary city bus, cracked vinyl seats and sallow, flickering, interior track lights, bounced along the wet narrow streets. Susanna sniffed, the pungent scent of diesel exhaust and sweat making her nose crinkle. She stared at the dingy bus interior, at the grimy, rain-streaked windows. It was as if the windows were caked in Vaseline, distorting the vague, lumbering shapes that moved with a strange lethargy along the glistening sidewalks. When the bus would jangle to a stop, Susanna would wipe the condensation from the dirt-caked window, press her forehead to the cool surface and peer outside. Dark and ragged shapes moved around in a wet world of faint blue light. It was a vague and hazy world to Susanna, as it had been since Kevin's disappearance. She realized she'd been looking for him; gazing out the dim windows in the equally dim hopes he'd be standing on the sidewalk, still and silent as a ghost, staring back at her. But Kevin wasn't out there waiting for her. He was still missing. Presumed dead. All Susanna saw was shadow upon shadow. And what did they see, she wondered, those hooded figures peering from the wet shadows?

In her more lucid moments she thinks, perhaps, that Kevin *is* out there among the shadows. That couldn't have been him there on the corner, could it? A frayed shadow-man who turned away from her when she'd glanced his way?

Susanna reached up and pulled the stop request cord. She stepped off the bus and into the cool rain. She fumbled in her purse for the red umbrella and managed to pluck it from the bottom of the bag and snap it open before her hair was spoiled, but not before she stepped into a puddle. Her feet were soaked, the shoes likely ruined. She mentally sighed, cursed the weather gods. She'd just had her hair done and would hate to see all that work, not to mention money, frittered away in mere moments. Not that Susanna had anywhere to go. She'd just needed to get out of the apartment. It was the first time she'd been to the salon since Kevin's disappearance. The first real, meaningful excursion into the city in a long while. She'd been sitting in the quiet apartment, trying to read a trashy paperback horror novel, but as was often the case lately, her thoughts drifted like smoke caught in a breeze, fragments dissipating and dissolving into nothing. Susanna sometimes thought her mind, like her thoughts, was like a ball of scratchy yarn, all the loose threads unravelling. She'd placed the book down, stood, went into the bathroom, and stared at herself in the mirror. It wasn't a pretty sight. She looked tired and grey. She *was* tired and grey. And her hair hung long and stringy and dull. So she'd made an appointment at a salon she hadn't frequented before, thus avoiding any contact and strained conversation with her usual hairstylist.

"How are you, Susanna? Haven't seen you in ages. How is Kevin?"

"Kevin's dead."

How else to explain it? If you told people Kevin was missing, it led to too many questions. And she could see the doubt, the *blame*, in their querulous expressions. It was easier this way, Susanna thought. *"Kevin is dead!"* It shut people up.

Now, standing in the chill rain, getting her hair done seemed such a petty and selfish thing. What was the point? She laughed grimly, and a passerby looked at her as if she was mad. And perhaps she was. She'd have thought the same thing if she saw a woman with sodden feet and a newly coiffed head, holding a red umbrella, and standing in the middle of the sidewalk cackling. Susanna decided, right then and there, that everyone was cursed with a little madness.

She and Kevin hadn't owned a car. They'd walk or take taxis. Sometimes they would roller-blade along the waterfront. They would get on the city bus and ride it through the various city blocks, watching each corner, each tiny part of the neighbourhood as it ceaselessly evolved. The city, she knew, was a live thing, a growing organism, feeding on its inhabitants.

Susanna recalled sitting on the bus with Kevin one summer day as it had rolled to a stop at a crowded intersection. Kevin had jostled her, pointed. "Look," he'd said.

She'd glanced to where Kevin indicated. A man (at least she'd thought the dim figure was a man by its bearing) and a small child in torn clothes were huddled beside a large wooden crate, partway down a narrow laneway. The man and child were passing something between them, each taking a bite before passing it back to the other. Susanna peered closer. What they shared appeared to be a bird of some sort. And it appeared to still be alive.

Then the bus had jerked away and Susanna turned to Kevin. "W-What was that?" she asked.

Kevin had sighed and answered cryptically, "It's all the things we never see."

That was Kevin, Susanna thought. Cryptic.

"If you open your eyes, Susanna," Kevin continued, "you'll see them."

Susanna had silently fumed for the rest of the bus ride.

The subway was their favourite mode of transportation. It was quick, efficient, and cheap. Why anyone would own a car in the city was a mystery to Susanna.

It was Kevin who introduced her to the joys of the subway: the clacking trains, the silver rails, the old stations tiled in fading shades of green and brown and ochre, and lit by hissing fluorescent tubes that threw luminous shadows along the platforms. She and Kevin would often take a day and ride the train to a selected station. It was a sense of adventure and discovery, coming up from the underground into a different world topside. Dark to light. Shadow to sunshine. At St. George station you found bistros and small cafes, specialty chocolate and jewellery shops, boutique hotels. Spadina station was Chinatown, where roast duck hung from hooks in every restaurant window, and where the sidewalks teemed with gawking tourists. Up the black steps from Osgoode station you emerged onto Queen Street, the West Village, a stretch of road that accommodated vintage clothing stores, Goth clubs, and music shops that still sold vinyl records. Each station stop was different, a new world unfolding before Susanna's eyes. She knew, though, that Kevin preferred exploring the stations below as much as the neighbourhoods. He liked the murky underbelly of the world. It was his job.

Kevin had been working on an investigative piece for *The Mirror*. He believed, had empirical evidence he'd said, of a hidden, long forgotten and little known, abandoned subway station, sealed off many years ago during the city's ambitious transit expansion. A subway station that now housed dozens, perhaps hundreds, of permanent residents who lived under the city.

"I'll find it, Susanna," Kevin had said. "Or they'll find me."

"They?" Susanna had asked.

Kevin had hunched forward, whispered, even though it was just the two of them in the apartment. "Them. The things below ground."

Susanna was taken aback. She hadn't noticed until then the dark rings around Kevin's eyes, his pale complexion. "*Things? If* there is a community of people living in the subway, they are still human, Kevin. Still like us."

"Hardly," Kevin said.

"Jesus, Kevin, get off it," Susanna had said. "You need to take a break."

"I'm close," he'd said. "So close."

And the next day he was gone, another soul lost to the hungry city.

She'd found a note scrawled on a small white card left in the center of the coffee table:

Open your eyes or you will be,
All the things we never see.

Susanna couldn't quite be sure, but the note did not appear to be in Kevin's handwriting.

The mechanical sound of the bus pulling away brought Susanna out of her reverie. She stepped off the sidewalk and ducked under a store awning. She glanced up and down the street, trying to get her bearings. It was an unfamiliar neighbourhood, and she wasn't sure where she was, wasn't even sure why she'd gotten off the bus before her stop.

Movement up ahead caught her eye. A shadow figure slipped around a corner, and before it dodged from sight it turned a pale face in her direction, and Susanna gasped. *Kevin?* Then she laughed again, because surely she was mad. It couldn't have been Kevin.

Nonetheless, Susanna started up the street after the dark phantom. As she had been since Kevin's disappearance, Susanna was caught up in twilight, that grey-haze of the day where day meets night. People, shapes really, slipped past her vision. She turned to gaze at them but it seemed they were always at the corners of her vision, distorted, as if viewed through a wide-angle lens that exaggerated features. Hers was a blurred reality.

Ahead, at the intersection of a small side street, Susanna noticed a large dark lump on the sidewalk. She shivered, slowed, moved cautiously toward the vague shape. When she reached the lumpy shape she stopped, looked down. The lump moved, slowly, as if awakening, and something like fear caught in her throat and fluttered madly there like a wild bird newly caged.

A pale face, all eyes and eager mouth, revealed itself from amongst the black tatters of a coat, and Susanna let out a held breath. Then she cackled again, and she believed that she just might be mad, after all. It wasn't Kevin. Of course not, she thought. Why would it be? *He was dead, don't fool yourself, kiddo.* Gone. But a part of her wondered, and she knew it always would.

The figure on the sidewalk thrust out a hand, grabbed Susanna's wrist, held tight. She tried to pull away, but couldn't break free from the powerful grip.

Since she'd found the note on the table, Susanna had tried to open her eyes, to *really* see. For the first time in her life she'd really looked. And she'd seen them, the people of the street, hunched and huddled and shivering, worn and tired, cold and hungry. They'd been there all along, she knew. And they always would be there, these material ghosts.

She'd opened her eyes and looked into *their* eyes. She saw pain and pride, regret and respect—all the things people carry through their short, unforgettable lives. Now that she could see them, she wouldn't ignore them. Kevin had been wrong; the street people were like everybody else. Like me, she thought. Like Kevin. All they needed was some help, someone to guide them. She could set them free.

Susanna leaned in, looked at the face of the slumped figure. It was a face like any other. "It's okay," she whispered. "I know. I know." She was amazed and mortified that before Kevin's disappearance she hadn't noticed the homeless. They were everywhere. Where did they come from? Where did they go?

The figure on the cracked sidewalk cocked its head, released its grip from Susanna's arm. She could smell wet leather. A strange gurgling sound came from somewhere within the wet clothes.

Susanna fished in her purse for her wallet. She opened it, plucked all the bills from it and pushed them into the figure's hand, as if money ever solved anything. At least, she thought, it could momentarily help this soul. "I'm sorry," she said. "Really." She was crying, but she didn't care. It was for Kevin, for the homeless, for everything. It was all coming out, finally. She hadn't cried in a very long time, and she wondered why people didn't cry more often. She shuddered at a society that promulgated crying as a weakness. She thought it was a brave thing to do.

She placed the bright red umbrella next to the slumped figure, canted it so it provided some shelter from the drizzle. Her hair would get wet, but it didn't matter. She didn't give a damn.

Susanna turned, glanced up the dreary street. Another dim figure stood further down the block, silent and still. Was it staring at her?

She moved up the street. The dark shape wavered, as if a mirage, seemed to shrink and hunch forward. Susanna blinked, and the figure slowly blended in with the brickwork and disappeared. A shadow-shape scuttled along the sidewalk and the wall, then slithered around the corner.

Heart racing, Susanna hurried forward, splashing through greasy puddles. She wasn't certain what she was chasing, but she felt sure it had something to do with Kevin. It was a message of some kind. A warning?

At the corner, Susanna stopped, peered down a slim, dark alley. Somewhere, a cat cried out and the wind pushed tin cans and plastic bags down the wet street. Something scuttled in the shadows. A rumble shook the ground, and Susanna glanced down to see she stood on a slotted grate. A rush of stale warm air billowed up from below and the rumble faded away. The subway.

Down the laneway she saw a gated entrance, a brick doorway. A lone sallow light lit the gate. That couldn't have been something wriggling through the gate, could it? Susanna couldn't tell if the squat dark shapes she saw were garbage cans... or something else. She walked down the graffiti-tagged alley. The trash cans were just trash cans and she was vaguely disappointed. Susanna reached the small brick alcove. A large padlock and heavy chain wrapped around the wrought iron.

Beyond the locked gate, wet, black stairs descended into darkness. The ground shook, and a smell like a wet blanket wafted up from below. Susanna leaned in, peered through the openings in the gate. She imagined gaunt, ashen faces and reaching limbs at the bottom of those dark stairs, and Kevin among them.

Susanna looked up, studied the gate for a way in. Then she saw it, above the alcove, spray-painted on the brick wall, a pair of wide, staring eyes, and below the eyes, in chunky block letters was written:

All the things we never see

The eyes were staring down, and Susanna saw the opening in the gate where one of the iron bars had been removed. It wasn't a very wide opening, but she figured she could slip through.

She doffed her wet coat and, arms first, pulled herself through the narrow breach. Susanna stood at the top of the stairs, letting her eyes adjust. Then she descended.

It wasn't as dark as it first appeared. At the bottom of the stairs was a large, empty hall, the walls curving up to form a vaulted ceiling. A wan light glowed, and Susanna could make out that the whole area was tiled in opalescent marble. An incessant drip echoed in the chamber. She began to walk, and her footsteps also echoed along the cavernous hall. A faint rumble shook the ground. Somewhere nearby a train passed, and in its wake she thought she heard a faint click-clacking echoing all around her, as if an army of mice marched along the damp tile.

The end of the cavern opened onto a train platform. In the dim light Susanna saw twin rails of silver running left and right, stretching into darkness. She smelled rotted fish and rancid milk. She stepped onto the platform, her feet sticking in a gummy residue. Other than the way she'd come in, Susanna could see no other exit so she shuffled forward along the platform. She peered left, then right, but the tunnels at either end were dark mysteries.

Susanna sensed something behind her, then there was a muffled clip-clopping sound. She wheeled around. At the opening to the great hall was a dark, stooped form holding a red umbrella.

She opened her mouth and whispered *Kevin*, but it came out in a strangled sibilance. Her feet tottered forward, toward the dim figure. The shape dropped the umbrella, appeared to hunch forward and wriggle along the wet platform, tiny limbs pulling it nearer. As it came closer, Susanna noticed its pale face was all eyes and mouth. It crawled, edging along the slick tiles, then stopped a few feet away from Susanna. The thing reared up on its back limbs, cocked its head, and regarded Susanna with a keen-eyed curiosity.

Susanna smiled. They weren't street people, after all. At least not entirely. They'd had to adapt down here, evolve. She stared at the tube-like body covered in tattered cloth, the short arms and legs that ended in malformed hands and feet, and the large, round eyes gazing at her. She saw something in those liquid eyes; a vast and wondrous spirit, a resilience. A silent plea for understanding. For help.

"My God," Susanna said, quaking, moving forward. "Such a wonder."

A distant rumble reverberated through the forgotten subway station. Susanna turned, saw a train emerge from the dark tunnel and roll up to the platform. All the cars were packed with shadowy shapes.

The train doors opened, and the creatures spilled onto the platform and wriggled toward Susanna. They gathered around her, all eyes trained on Susanna, silent and expectant.

Susanna turned, round and round, trying to meet their eyes. She spread her arms. "Oh," she said, "all the things we never see."

They bore her aloft, shunted her atop their nubby, claw-like appendages, their sallow, wrinkled faces and bulbous eyes turned towards her in reverence, their thin, wide mouths grinning. And Susanna was only too happy to let them pass her around... until they began to nip at her with their sharp little teeth.

Eight Haiku

damp October leaves
boneless blood-wet tissue skins
Death's fragrant perfume

brush of ruby lips
fleshy nape of virgin neck
delicate demon

fat black lonesome crow
thin grey wedge of open sky
the day flies away

silent boardwalk dreams
foggy finger tendrils drift
cool night rushes in

shimmering Green wood
I whistle softly and a
little fairy comes

phantom figure smiles
cool whispering wind crackles
swinging scythe cries out

pneumatic clicking
metallic spider dropping
strands of silken web

they come out at night
slow summer wings fluttering
mad moths to a flame

Different Skins

Gary had no use for ghosts.

"They covered her over with mud and sticks," Will said.

Carmen sipped her beer, licked the foam off her lips, and placed the glass on the scarred wooden table. "That's awful," she said.

Gary had been transfixed by Carmen's small pink tongue, the way it circled her.

Will punched Gary's arm. "Wake up," Will said. "I was talking to you."

Gary shrugged. Will was always talking, telling stories. When Gary had first arrived at the University of Toronto, Will would try to sit near him and Carmen in Philosophy 101. The three of them were new to the University, new to the city. Chatty Will had struck up conversations with them. Since then, they spent a good amount of their evenings together at the University's Hart House Pub. Gary went along because of Carmen. She seemed enthralled with Will's tall tales.

"Sorry," Gary said. "I'm a little pre-occupied. What were you saying?"

"Ghosts," Carmen said. "We were talking about ghosts. Don't you ever pay attention, Gary?" Carmen chided. "Even in Philosophy class, every time I turn around you're daydreaming. Or staring at me."

Gary blushed, hoped it didn't show in the dim light. He swallowed some beer, said "Some of us are talkers, some of us are thinkers."

Will and Carmen exchanged a look; they laughed.

Gary flushed again, this time with anger.

Carmen said, "Sheesh, relax, Gary. We're not trying to take the piss out of you."

Gary had faces, like skins, like personalities, for every occasion. If you could put on a face, you could get whatever you wanted. He tried on his most sincere face, stared at Carmen, unblinking. "Sorry, C, you're right." He glanced at Will. "Go on, Will. Start again. I'm listening."

Will sighed. "Sure," he said. "I'm going to tell you about the ghost of Taddle Creek. The Lady of the Sticks. You both know

Philosopher's Walk, don't you?"

Carmen nodded.

"Of course," Gary said. Philosopher's Walk was the large green space that meandered over much of the University's campus. It was mostly lawn and trees and scenic footpaths. If Gary had no use for ghosts, he had even less use for parks and songbirds. He didn't come to the city to get back to nature. He stared at Carmen. She was looking at Will, expectant, waiting. Her aquiline profile and pouty lips were perfect. No, Gary thought, she's the reason I came to the city. You didn't see girls like Carmen in Wilkie, Saskatchewan.

"It's a little-known fact," Will continued, "that the footpaths of Philosopher's Walk follow what was once a small river called Taddle Creek. There are traces of it still, along the walk. The small ravine bordering the path is what's left of the creek. The ghost of Taddle Creek haunts Philosopher's Walk. She's a young woman, 21 or 22 years old, our age, who drowned in the creek in the 1880's.She's been spotted on the footpaths, dressed in denim coveralls dripping water. Her hair is cut short, in a fashion that suited the men of that era. Some have said her skin is translucent green, covered in algae, and that at night you can see her essence moving along the various footpaths, like some macabre lantern. Leeches and moss crawl along her green skin. Sometimes people have seen what looks like wet footprints appearing and disappearing on the paths, followed by the sounds of rushing water and strange gurgles.

"Other eyewitnesses have said she isn't green at all, but is a creature of mud and sticks, shambling along the footpaths at night, as if she is searching for something."

Gary snickered. "Yeah, a hot bath."

Carmen shot Gary a withering look. He was about to apologize, then thought *Fuck it, it's only a joke. When did the world get so serious, so damn politically correct?*

"Why?" Carmen asked. "Why is she here, haunting the campus?"

Will leaned toward Carmen. She inched closer to Will, looked at him all dreamy-eyed. It was as if Gary weren't even there. As if he didn't exist at all. He might as well be back in Wilkie.

"Do you believe in ghosts?" Will asked. Carmen nodded, uttered a breathy "yes."

Will turned to Gary. "What about you?"

Gary shrugged, said "Not really. Do you, Will? You believe all this stuff?"

"Yes," Will said. "I do. I've seen her, The Lady of the Sticks, once, very briefly, late at night, sloshing along the creek bed, a walking bramble of sticks and thorns. It was early one morning. I was getting a run in before classes. I saw movement down in the little gulley, so I stopped running, walked to the edge of the footpath. I thought, perhaps, there was a coyote or groundhog or something down by the creek. Peering down, I didn't see anything, at first. Then a figure appeared to separate from the bank of the culvert, materializing from the mud, and tottered along the creek bed. I blinked. It was early, I'd not eaten, and I was breathing heavy from the run. I'd convinced myself I was seeing things. But the stick creature seemed to sense my presence, and it turned, slowly. Though it hadn't a proper face, it stared right at me, dark hollows for eyes. I saw a mouth, stuffed with mud, moving noiselessly in the middle of that dark countenance. It cocked its head, as if sizing me up, then turned back—with a forlorn resignation, I thought—to the creek. It trundled up the shallow bed of water and disappeared around the bend. In hindsight, it seemed a pitiable thing."

"Wow," Carmen said. "Incredible. Nothing like that has ever happened to me."

Will smiled at Carmen. "I got the distinct impression it was searching for something. That it wanted something from me. Some sort of help, perhaps. It was trying to tell me something, but its mouth and throat were clogged with dirt."

Gary grinned. He knew what Will was doing. He was trying on a different skin, one that would impress Carmen. He knew the game and could play along. "Impressive story, Will," Gary said.

Will frowned. "It's true."

Gary drummed his fingers on the scarred tabletop. "Of course," he said.

Carmen glanced at Gary, turned back to Will. "You found out

what it was?"

"Bet you did some research on it, eh, Will?" Gary said.

"Yes," Will said. "After the experience on the footpath, I started poking around the reference library, looking at old newspaper clippings, books, etc. Here's what I discovered.

"It was the 1880's," Will said. "Times were tough. It was a hard world, especially for a single woman looking for work." He took a swallow of beer. "There was a city work crew commissioned to bury Taddle Creek and convert it to an underground sewer system. Pretty advanced stuff for the time.

"Anyway," Will continued, "it was a big project, and everyone in the city knew about it.

"One day this young man shows up at the work site, looking for the foreman. This *man* is young, scrawny, dressed in overalls, his hair cut straight and short; a billed-cap on his head protects his face from the sun, and from the curious crew."

Will stopped, slurped some beer. The ambient noise of the pub; hushed conversations, clinking glasses, and raucous laughter, buffeted their table like some live thing. Will cast an inquisitive glance at Gary and Carmen. Gary thought Will's gaze lingered overly long on Carmen.

Will grinned, said "Of course our thin young man with the strange haircut wasn't a man, at all, but a young woman posing as a man to try and find gainful employment."

"Of course," Gary muttered. "That's what women do."

Carmen glared.

Gary tried on one of his many faces. "A joke, Carmen. Just a joke."

Carmen looked away.

"Anyway," Will continued, "the young lady was of independent spirit. She'd come from a small town to the big city to make her mark." Will turned to Gary. "Like you, Gare."

Gary hated to be called 'Gare.' He conjured his Cheshire cat face, the one that promised to eat you alive, fixed it on Will. "Whatever you say, Will." Then, to himself: *Always. Whatever you say.*

"Taddle Creek is the biggest construction project in the city,"

Will said. "It's ambitious, and even though times are tough, as they are now, day labourers are needed to help get the city's new sewer system done in a timely fashion." He sipped flat beer. "So, suitably disguised, our young lady is handed a shovel and hired."

"How did she pass for a man?" Carmen asked.

Gary forced a smile. "It's easy. We all have different skins."

Carmen blinked at him. Gary continued smiling at her until she looked away.

"That's the tragedy," Will continued. "One day, the men in the crew found out there was a woman in their midst. Maybe her hat slipped off. Maybe there was something decidedly different about her movements, her size, and her voice, how she carried herself. Who knows? Either way, the crew found out. And they were none too happy."

Will looked at Carmen. "Back then," he said, "men were inherently crueler to women."

"Not much different these days," Carmen said.

Gary couldn't be sure, but he thought Carmen's eyes flicked his way.

"Apparently," Will continued, "this happened near the completion of the sewer system. One of the last days. There'd been some test runs. So the men decided they would have some fun with the poor woman. It was a Friday. Pay day. Near the end of her shift, the foreman sent her down into the belly of sewer with a shovel. She was told to literally shovel shit, keep it moving."

Like you, Will, Gary thought. *You and your tall tales. Shovelling shit.*

Will rubbed his chin, blinked, and moved closer to Carmen. "So the young lady went down the hatch, hauling a shovel. Once she was down there, though, they closed all the hatches, locked them. The men thought they would put a fright into her, keep her down there in the dark, wet, and smelly sewer."

Carmen shuddered. "I can't imagine," she said.

"Truly appalling," Gary said, feigning disgust.

"The crew had a good chuckle, then decided to break for lunch. What harm could there be if she spent an hour or so down there? So they headed to the nearest pub, money in their pockets, and proceeded to partake of the local establishment's libations. Hours later, drunk and lighter of pocket, they trundled back to the work site. It was only upon returning that they recalled they'd left the woman down there. So they unlocked the hatches and waited for her to come up. But she didn't emerge from the darkness. Nothing did. At least not right away.

"Eventually a few of the men went down the hatch. They stumbled about blindly in the semi-darkness, calling. And they found her, nearly tripped over her, half-buried in a pile of mud and sticks, her mouth agape as if she were trying to scream or catch one last, desperate breath. Dead."

Carmen trembled. "O-Oh, my," she said.

Gary thought Carmen was going to cry. He grinned unpleasantly.

"The crew decided they would leave her down there. They figured no one knew about her. She was a day labourer and the records, if any, were spotty at best. So the men in the sewer pushed her body into the mud and covered her over until there was no trace of her.

"As far as we know, she is buried there still. Only her spirit walks along the paths of the campus. Her bones are deep in the mud."

"A mouthful of mud," Carmen said. "Silenced forever."

Gary thought about putting something in Carmen's mouth.

Will reached over, patted Carmen's hand. "Yes."

Gary sighed.

"What is it?" Will asked.

"Nothing, Will. It's a good story. You like telling stories."

"You're not convinced?" Carmen asked.

"No," Gary said. "It's all nonsense. Mumbo jumbo."

"There were news accounts of a missing Toronto woman," Will said. "And mentions of an industrial accident during the final days of the sewer's construction. I've pieced this account together from various sources."

"I'm sure you have," Gary said. "It's the ghost stuff. Hocus-pocus. I don't believe it."

"But I've seen her," Will said. "So have others."

Gary groaned. "*I* haven't."

"Not yet," Carmen said. "Maybe we should look for her."

Gary was about to mock Carmen's idea when he caught himself and slipped another skin on. "That's a great idea, Carmen," he said. His voice was treacle. This was an opportunity to show her that he was every bit the man Will was, and more. "I'll go one better. I'll spend the night down in the gulley. If this stick ghost is down there, I'll find her."

"Why on earth would you do that?" Carmen asked.

Gary shrugged, smiled. "Why not? I'll go to the source. Try to prove you right, Will." *Or wrong*, he thought.

Carmen and Will looked at him. "Sure," Will said. "This'll be a fun exercise. When?"

Gary stared at Carmen until she glanced away. "Tomorrow," he said.

Gary was wearing a different skin today. It was thick and tough. Impenetrable. Like him. It registered on his face, where a half-sneer perched like a leashed predator.

Carmen, Will, and Gary stood on the curving path of Philosopher's Walk. Save for a few straggling late-night students, the campus was empty. Parallel to the path was a small trickle of water, the remnants of Taddle Creek. The creek snaked slowly through a culvert of high, muddy banks. The culvert twisted away, around a bend, south, through a stand of elms and oaks, toward Toronto proper, to empty into the vast and frigid Lake Ontario.

Will pointed. "Down there," he said. "That's where she's buried. In the mud. The creek banks were the sewer walls."

It was dusk, the sky blue-black. The sodium lights along the path, at least the ones that hadn't been smashed by vandals or drunken frat boys, threw garish orange light along the walkway. The creek and muddy culvert disappeared in the encroaching darkness.

"Okay, then," Gary said, flicking on his flashlight, "off I go."

"How will we know if you find her?" Carmen asked.

"I'll tell you, won't I?" Gary said.

Will shuffled forward. "Even if you don't see her, it doesn't prove anything."

Gary frowned. "Well, I'm willing to give it a try. That's something, isn't it?"

"It's true, Will," Carmen said. "He's open to it so cut him some slack."

Gary smiled. This was brilliant, this concerned sensitive type. He'd have to wear this skin more often. Tomorrow, he'd be golden.

Will scratched his head. "Sure. Of course. Good luck, Gare."

"Adieu," Gary said, then turned with a flourish and, sweeping the flashlight before him, moved along the path, down the bank and splashed into shallow Taddle Creek. He stopped, looked back, saw Carmen and Will watching him, so waved and hurried through the creek-bed and around the bend. Out of sight, he climbed back up the muddy creek bank and squatted. He'd wait half an hour, give Carmen and Will time to get back to the residence, then he'd take the rear footpath along the campus back to his dorm. Then, in the morning, he'd wake early, throw the muddy clothes back on, and sneak back down to the creek, where Carmen and Will would find him.

He smiled. It was a good plan. Ghosts, he thought. He had no use for them. He had even less use for Will. Always glomming onto Carmen. Always talking. You couldn't shut him up. A mouthful of dirt would keep him quiet.

Gary lay back on the bank, stretched. He turned off the flashlight. It wasn't quite dark yet. The sky was a shifting mass of pearled clouds. The wind pushed them south, toward the lake. And the night-wind sang through the autumn trees, low and sad. Another sound reached Gary's ears; a slow gurgle of water. The creek. Then a sloshing sound like some *thing* moving through the shallow water, slow and deliberate.

He sat up, blinked. Momentarily, Gary thought he saw a dim shadow move across the creek-bed. Then that gurgling sound again, only this time it came from behind him, and it was more of a gasping or choking sound. He was about to peer around when two figures crested the creek bank opposite him. He squinted into the near dark.

Carmen and Will. They were holding hands, staring down at him, silent as ghosts.

Gary tried to stand, but he'd been squatting too long in the same spot and his feet had sunk deep into the mud and were stuck. He attempted to pull a leg free, but he only sank further. The ground below him shifted, rippled, made a wet sucking sound. Gary put his hands on the ground to try and get some leverage and boost himself free. His hands sank into the runny mud. It seemed as if the ground pulled at them greedily.

On the other bank, the two figures hugged, blending into one shadowy shape. *Why aren't they helping me?* Gary thought. "Hey," he called. "Down here."

The ancient wind moaned, moved along the creek-bed. The air thrummed, smelled of dead leaves. The ground swelled, pulsed as if alive, and lapped at Gary. He struggled, and fell further into the moving mud.

"Help!"

Beneath Gary something hard and angular poked through the mud, as if he were laying on a pile of broken twigs or a heap of bones. The bone-sticks broke through the ground and two appendages encircled him like the arms of a long-lost lover.

"Help."

Gary writhed. And the mud and bone thing pulled. He sank. He opened his mouth to scream and mud and sticks filled his mouth. The further he descended into the creek bank, the more the black mud crawled over him. And just before he sank beneath the surface, he was nothing more than a skin of mud.

Hand in hand, Will and Carmen turned away, walked along the footpath back toward the campus. Carmen looked at Will, half-smiled, squeezed Will's hand, said, "Life is full of sacrifices, Will. There's nothing to feel bad about. You helped her. Set her free. Sacrificed one to save many."

Will grinned. "Oh, I don't feel bad about it. He was always

talking about people having different skins. He's wearing a new one now, I suppose."

"In a way," Carmen said, "he was right. We do have different skins. Some of us don't wear them on the outside."

Will leaned over, kissed Carmen on the mouth. "Amen to that," he said.

Down the footpath, around the bend, through a shallow creek-bed, and up a muddy creek bank, something stirred. A dark, vaguely humanoid shape wrenched itself free of the creek bank. It stood in darkness, blinked dirt-encrusted eyes, to be met with darkness still. It opened a mud-filled mouth, but no sound emanated from that dark maw. Then the mud-thing turned and shambled blindly through the shallow water, its black mouth issuing screams that no one could hear.

Tears from an Eyeless Face

You wake to sudden silence and stygian darkness; black and quiet like a country coffin buried deep in the earth.

You've lived in the same small apartment, (a tiny, musty box shoe-horned beside other boxes and placed inside a bigger box) in the same grim neighborhood in the same bland city for a very long time. You've walked the same cracked and sorrowful streets, devoid of sunshine and birdsong, shuffling past the same sad citizens—their faces runny grey blurs—for countless years. You shuffle among them, unnoticed, another grey blob on life's large grey canvas.

You've worked the same menial job. You watch endless reruns on the ancient, fuzzy Zenith television. You eat the same frozen grey dinner, your mouth like ash.

Only now, late in your forlorn life, you take an interest in painting. But you wake this day to discover you have no eyes. Though you once had eyes, you have, in truth, always been blind.

To paint, you think, would have been to love.

Only now, in your last desolate days, you take an interest in song. But you wake this day to discover you have no mouth. Though you once had a mouth, you have, in truth, mostly been mute.

To sing, you think, would have been to love.

And only now, in your lost life, you take an interest in music. But you wake this day to discover you have no ears. Though you once had ears, you have, in truth, always been deaf.

To make music, you think, would have been to love.

You've woken this day to discover you have no face.

You wake this day alone. You have always been alone. And now you are blind, deaf, and mute. The blind see more than you; the deaf hear more than you; the mute speak louder.

You wake this day to discover you have no life.

Only now, on your last desolate day, you take an interest in touch.

You still have hands. You lift them to your head and touch what is left of your face. It is wet, clammy and uneven, like a lump of malleable grey clay.

You wonder what it would have been like to kiss someone; to fall in love; to hold hands. In the black room, you flex your fingers and wonder again what it would have been like to paint, to create, to sit at an easel, a canvas, and cover it in thick paint, thick love. Thick wet love.

Wet.

Your face is wet, runny. Like a daub of grey paint. You are crying. Tears streaming down an eyeless face.

You stand, stumble to the bare living room wall. You move your fingers, hold them to your face, cup it as if it is a ball of wet clay. You rub your non-face, cover your fingers in thick wet love.

You press your hands to the wall and begin to paint.

The White-Face
at Dawn

A scarlet dawn breaches the thick gloom of the apartment. Slender pink fingers of thin light rouse me from another restless night, plagued by fever-dreams of dear Genevieve, and dreams of the curious tatter-king in yellow robes, a grey and gaunt being that clutches a sceptre of black onyx and wears a crown of tarnished jewels upon his thorny head. His is a face of dark cunning and sharp angles. Grave-worm tongue. It was he, I'm sure, who came for Genevieve.

A noise, as well, gave me fits through the night. A sound like thick clomping, as if the tenant upstairs had traversed their apartment in wooden clogs. *Clomp!... clomp!... clomp!*

I am on the small divan in the main room. The bedroom door is closed—the bedroom I had shared with sweet Genevieve and her eyes likes sunshine, skin like alabaster, lips like the ripest fruit. Her voice, her song, was like a choir of angels. All gone, now. Gone forever. Her outer beauty hid an inner weakness, a faulty heart. And now it is I who is stricken with the broken heart. Oh, Genevieve, my lost love. I have not had the courage to go back to the bedroom, our bed, our former life.

Rising up, blinking, the night's unease slowly dissipates, leaving with it a taste of wormwood. I move to the window, throw it open to the rosy dawn and peer out into the cobbled square struggling to wake, like all the denizens of the starving city.

In the square, vendors uncover burlap stalls, their wares made ready. The grand marble fountain sits idle. Old women, veiled in black, waddle across the stonework like fat pigeons. The air smells of turpentine. A faint yellow haze hangs in the brightening sky.

Presently, movement in the square catches my eye. I lean out; peer across to the terraced balconies on the other side of the square. Shadows and shadows, dark upon dark. The dual fledgling suns will not reach these quarters until late afternoon. It is why I chose the westerly side—my best work is done in soft morning light.

Again there is furtive movement from the shadows opposite. Then I see it, and draw back alarmed; a white-white face, bright as bleached parchment and smooth as a mask of exquisite marble, wan and pallid, a frozen stoicism.

A white-face at dawn.

The visage unnerves me; blank and staring, an impassive and patient perfection, its simple lack of expression somehow conveying a terrible beauty. I am reminded of the work of young Boris Yvain, and I shudder and step back into the shadows of my room, away from that judging face.

I shake my head, trying to release the fog of night. Ah, Boris, I think. There is beauty in stone, but always the cracks will appear.

I try to put the white-face out of my mind. I move into the kitchenette and make a meagre breakfast of coffee, and toast smothered in marmalade. Work beckons, so I bring the meal into the drawing room and sit at my desk. I gaze at the closed bedroom door. In the gap between the floor and the door edge I think I see something. Movement perhaps. Something stirring. But then I blink and I see nothing but a wedge of darkness seeping under the door. I shake my head and look back at my desk.

From the desk drawer I retrieve my tools—parchment, ink, and quills—and place them at the ready. I will create a masterpiece, something more magnificent even than *The King in Yellow*, that pellucid and unforgettable creation that enervates and terrifies me so. Mine will be the book that they snatch from the stalls and read at night by flickering lamplight. They will sing my praises. Mine will be the glory.

Gazing up, my eyes drift to the corner of the room. The manikin, a remnant of my former life, stares impassively, judging. I smile, recalling many wonderful times when I would finish a garment on the manikin and then fit it to Genevieve; the dressing, then the undressing. Then, inevitably, to the bedroom where we would luxuriate in the silks, the satins, and our skin. Perhaps, I think, I should be rid of the old thing. It is but another arrow in my heart.

I turn back to the parchment, my new life, sip my thick coffee and begin, but after a few attempts I stutter. The words will not come. The muse is elusive. I press on, but all I scratch into the parchment seems an illogical and convoluted mess. After a time I admit defeat and retreat to the balcony. Perhaps the beckoning suns will light something inside of me.

I think of the white-face. The balconies across the way are still shrouded in darkness. I gaze intently at the shadows. I see faint glimmers of pale lamplight leaking from some of the apartments. And movement. The occupants, I think, stirring behind shuttered windows and closed blinds. I try to recall from which balcony the white-face loomed. I blink. Was it directly across from me? Below? To the right? My memory fails. It could have been anywhere. Suddenly I have a vision of the white-face crawling across the edifice of the building, over balconies, across windows, herbody—and I am certain it is a 'she'—fast and agile, her head smooth, smiling stone.

These drear thoughts cloud my mind. I will not be getting any work done soon, so decide upon a walk.

The square is filled with frenetic movement and loud chatter; orange sunlight and blue shadows. I smell fresh bread and honey. At a rickety stall I buy a croissant from a short, dark man. "Good day," I say to the stout man, smiling, trying to be upbeat, but he only grunts in return. The croissant is stale, tough, but I decide I will not let anything else adversely affect my mood. Genevieve would have smiled and carried on.

Men, women, and children swirl past me in a steady blur. I am the one still thing in a world of motion; the centre, the apex, an inhabitant of Carcosa. Without Genevieve, I am alone. I feel faint, dizzy. I stumble to the nearest cafe table and fall into an empty seat. I close my eyes to try to quell the spinning world.

Eyes closed, I "see" it again—the white-face. Smooth, stoic stone swimming in my vision, floating in the darkness. I start, open my eyes, and gasp.

At my feet something black scuttles across the dark cobblestones. A spider, thin and long-legged, perhaps sensing my sudden attention, stands still as a statue on the warm brickwork. I stand and quickly bring my boot heel down on the black creature. I imagine a satisfying crunch, but it does not come. When I lift my foot there is no trace of the spider.

I stumble blindly across the plaza into a small back alley. I lean against the cool, dark alley wall, panting and blinking. Perhaps, like the white-face, I simply imagined the spider. Perhaps I imbibed too much absinthe last night. It would not be the first time. Or the last.

I try to recall the evening, but it is as elusive as my muse is. I have a faint recollection of a woman, though, which is impossible. There was but one woman for me—Genevieve. There will be no other.

The alley is dark and narrow. It smells of fish guts and despair. I think I hear something, a noise like the clicking of tiny feet along the damp cement of the alleyway. A scuttling. Then a soft whoosh, like the exhalation of a held breath. Perhaps a stuttering, muffled clomp. I imagine movement at the end of the alley, a stirring. I lean forward, squint. I take one stuttering step forward, then another. "H-Hello?" I say. I cannot be sure, but I think I see a pale shape move out of the shadows, a head, or rather a pallid mask, staring sightlessly. Clutching my head, I turn and race out of the alley, vowing to quit the drink once and for all. It would not be the first time.

Then I wake on the small divan in my apartment. The bedroom door is closed—the bedroom I had shared with dear Genevieve. I am tired, and my head is clouded in thick fog. My sleep was fitful. There was a strange noise during the night, a clomping sound, as if the occupant of the apartment above me was wearing wooden shoes. My body itched and prickled all night. I am uncertain what day it is. But I did not drink; I am sure of it.

Rising, I am momentarily startled to discover a figure standing in the corner, silent and still as a winter night. I move forward, hand outstretched, and blink. It is the manikin, naked and immobile, its lower half nothing more than three bare wooden pegs like a saloon stool; its upper half a female torso, its ghastly pink-white skin a patina of cracks and spider-lines, peeling paint. In the dim morning light I discern the face of the manikin. The black eyes stare, unblinking, the mouth open in a grim rictus. I imagine I hear a scream issuing from that unmoving black maw. The head is bald, smooth and glowing like the strange moons above the city.

I recall the old profession; the tailoring and garment-mending, the fine silks and satins, the buttons, needles and pins, the dressing and undressing. Especially the dressing and undressing. I smile. Before Genevieve, there were many women in need of mending. I had, at that time, quite the reputation; one in need of repair.

I shuffle forward and reach out to stroke the manikin's cheek, but I stop. There is a black spot on the ancient manikin's cheek that is moving, crawling slowly across the cracked and broken skin. Another damnable spider! It perches by the manikin's mouth, as if it has crawled from that black hole. I strike the creature with my open hand, squishing it. It leaves a dark smear on the peeling paint. For a moment, I think I hear a small scream emanate from the manikin.

Unnerved, I turn from the still manikin. The apartment is quiet, the windows and drapes closed. I totter toward the bedroom, but the closed door mocks me, stops me in my tracks. I stare at the door. A drear unease settles in me. I back away from the bedroom, grab my waistcoat, and flee the apartment.

Outside, in the light, I look up into the twin suns. By their placement, I guess it to be the mid-afternoon. But how can that be, I think, surely I haven't slept through all the morning?

So it is that I presently find myself outside the Four Winds Pub, squinting up at the wooden sign over the thick black door. I have no recollection of what happened when I departed my apartment, no recollection of how I got here, for now the suns are descending and the afternoon wanes.

I pull open the heavy door and enter. The air is thick with smoke and conversation. Old Viktor is at the bar, so I make my way over.

"Hail," Old Viktor says to me. "My, but you are looking a bit put out. Yours is a face of worries and sorrows, my old friend."

I'm dimly aware that I haven't eaten, but before I can order a plate of food Old Viktor is placing a double dram in front of me. "On the house," he says. "You look like you need it."

I down the whisky in one gulp and as I place the glass back on the counter I see it, a spider, crawling drunkenly across the moist, dark wood. Furious, I raise my hand to strike at the creature but Old Viktor grabs my arm.

"No," he says, "you mustn't kill the spider. They carry our sorrows. It is considered bad form and will bring you ill luck."

I lower my hand and stare at Old Viktor. "My luck could not be any worse," I say.

"Perhaps," Old Viktor says. Then, "Do you know the story of the Sorrow Spiders?"

I shake my head morosely.

"Come then," he says, leaving the counter to Young Viktor and directing me to a far dark table, but not before getting us both a large dram. "Perhaps this will be good fodder for your next book.

"I heard this tale from Hawberk the Armourer," Old Viktor says, "who heard it from Severn. But it is as true an account as you'll hear.

"A long time ago, well before Carcosa had towers, quays, and bridges, when the black stars dripped misery, there lived a young man, Gaston, the son of the great sculptor Vance. Gaston was in love with an equally young maiden, Camilla.

Now, Vance was no ordinary sculptor. It was said, in fact, that his art was the product of dark magick. With a touch and an invocation, he could turn animate objects to stone. Gaston was a falconer, but was said to have a menagerie of pets, and was particularly fond of spiders. Spiders, Gaston claimed, were of the living world and the dead. Thus, they could travel between worlds, transporting souls. They could even, on rare occasion, reanimate the dead."

Here, Old Viktor paused to take a sip of whisky. I did the same.

Old Viktor continued. "Vance had forbidden Gaston to see Camilla, a commoner. The truth was that Camilla was such a young beauty that Vance secretly desired her to himself. He was a man who was used to getting what he wanted. But the young lovebirds continued their affair, unabated, infuriating Vance.

"Then, one day, when Camilla went to Lake Hali to meet her lover, she found, instead, a man of stone, smooth and dead, perched beneath a great, weeping willow. Camilla was cleft with grief. She was inconsolable. She wept for hours by the bank of the lake, holding tight to the cold stone. Finally, too overcome to continue, Camilla flung herself into Lake Hali. But, after some time, the lake threw her back onto shore. She wasn't dead, but she wasn't quite alive, either.

"Though Gaston had been turned to solid stone, spiders began to emerge from his mouth. Hundreds of them spilled from him and skittered down to the lakeshore where they crawled atop the unconscious form of Camilla and entered her open mouth. It is said that they were drawn to her grief, her pain. She was trapped in some sort of purgatory, a no-man's land, and the spiders offered safe passage on her journey, wherever that would take her."

I shuffle nervously in my chair and down the rest of my whisky. "And?" I say.

Old Viktor smiles. "She rose up, of course. This half-dead, half alive woman, dripping wet, shambled across the countryside to the home of Vance, the renowned sculptor. She found him in his studio. When Vance saw her, he stood, expecting angry recriminations. But Camilla only smiled wide and shuffled forward. Black things moved in her mouth. She smiled wider and stuttered toward Vance. *Could it be?* Vance thought. *Did she want me all this time?* Camilla opened her arms. 'Come close,' she said. 'I want to give you a kiss.' And Vance moved to her and put his greedy mouth on hers, and Camilla, seemingly with the strength of stone and grief, held him tight as the spiders moved from her to him, filling him and filling him to bursting as he struggled against the black surge."

My stomach is queasy. "Quaint story," I say.

"They found Vance days later," Old Viktor says, "prone on the studio floor, his face a frozen mask of terror. They blamed it on his heart troubles. A weak heart, they said. The statue of his son, Gaston, was also in the studio, as if it had miraculously 'come alive' and walked the countryside, as well. There was a nest of spiders in his black mouth."

I cough. "And the girl? Camilla?"

"They didn't find her. She was never seen again. Now, though, she is said to visit upon those who mourn lost loved ones. Their sorrows attract her. They feed her, keep her tethered to this world. She is said to take the form of a large spider, with the face of a beautiful young woman. A face, they say, that could only be made of pure white stone."

Dizzy, I stand. I think I should eat, but it seems imperative that I should get home without further delay. I wave aside Old Viktor's ministrations and hurry out of the pub.

The black stars drip, as if weeping. In the dark, under the strange moons, I find my way home.

In the apartment, heart-racing, I move to the bedroom door. *Oh, Genevieve.* My eyes well up with heavy tears. Then, still dizzy and faint from lack of food, I stumble over and fall onto the divan. Then, everything goes black.

I'm awakened by an odd noise, a muffled *clomp, clomp.* I sit up on the divan and blink. My eyes go to the closed bedroom door. *Clomp.* There it is again. Clomp. It is coming from the other side of the room.

Clomp.

I stand.

Clomp... clomp.

I shuffle forward. Then, as my eyes adjust to the dim light, I see it, the manikin, pale and ghostly, limned in moonlight, moving toward me, its wooden legs skidding along the floor in a herky-jerky dance. Something black is moving inside the manikin's mouth. Then, a sound from the bedroom, a strange scuttling, and I whip my head toward the door. In the gap between the door edge and the floor I see movement, a blacker black, and a wedge of darkness seeping under the door and scurrying towards me, a chitinous rush of black noise. And the manikin dance. *Clomp... clomp.*

Then, beyond the bedroom, that noise again, a whoosh, like an exhaled breath, and a rustling, as if someone or something is stirring from a deep rest, rising, coming out of the bedroom pale and smiling and whispering "*Come here and give me a kiss.*"

Turn the Page

It's coming for her, she hears it, far off but drawing nearer, the flutter and flap of ancient wings. Angel, demon, or something else—she doesn't yet know. Its story, like many, is yet to be told. If only she had the time.

Edith is old. She is dying. She hasn't always been old, but, like everyone, she's always been dying. And she's always been alone, her only company books and words. Books and words were her grand adventure. Some small solace in a world of mute sorrows.

Edith sits at her battered desk beside the window in her cramped apartment. She gazes out the grimy window to a sooty world, with grey thoughts in her head, and though the view has changed somewhat in the past thirty-three years, Edith hasn't. Not much, at any rate. She's just gotten old. Long ago she dreamed in colour, she dreamed adventure. Now she dreams in shades of grey; a wan and pallid world, paper thin. Edith can hear the wings flapping in time to her heart, slow and slower. It's coming for her. It's almost time. Some company at last, she thinks. At the very end.

Edith's heart is indeed slowing. She can feel it. *Thump-thump. Thump...* Her mind, too. She is winding down like some archaic clockwork piece—*tick... tick*—the springs and wheels rusting and breaking down, stopping. Ending. *Tick.* Well, Edith thinks, every story needs an ending.

Her ending, like her life, will be a quiet one, alone and unnoticed, unimportant, the great world spinning, the cosmos unaffected, order retained. The world will be no better or worse off with or without her. The universe has no need for legacies. After all, what did she contribute? What will she leave behind? Nothing but a few books; some writings of little import. Edith grimaces, sighs, wipes her suddenly wet eyes with a palsied hand.

With some effort she reaches up, unhooks the clasp and pushes the window up. A damp wind seeps into the apartment; dead leaves, blackest earth, a hint of regret, a touch of sorrow. Who doesn't have regrets?, she thinks. Or sorrows? Perhaps, if she were to start again, she wouldn't be so alone. Perhaps.

She leans out and looks down. It's a long way down. So far down. Far enough, Edith knows. She leans further out, listening, waiting as the great world slows and something draws nearer.

Edith turns back to the desk, picks up her pen and presses the nub to the blank page—white and glaring—then, with a shaking hand, begins. Her hand steadies. The words flow indigo. She writes, scrawls sentences long and short, poetic and prosaic. She turns the pages, their sound like wings drawing ever nearer, like the slowing of a clockwork heart. The wind gusts through the window, damp, with a trace of frost.

Blue lines on a white page. The pages turning. Her hand moves and her mind wanders. She is Alice in the looking glass. She is Dorothy in Oz. She is Peter Pan, Captain Hook, and John Carter. She is Lucy in the wardrobe. She has been to Treasure Island and Mars. She's been to Hogwarts and Camelot, Castlerock and Discworld. She is Oliver and Fagan, Moll Flanders and Pippi Longstocking. She is everything and everybody, and she's been on a grand adventure.

Done, Edith puts down the pen and closes the book. She traces her fingers over the cover, along the spine. She lifts it to her face, breathes in its essence; cracked leather, tattered parchment, blood, sweat, and many tears. Close now, so close, she hears the wings beating like some giant page in the heavens or a canvas flap in the star-studded night-sky opening to other worlds. She stands by the window, leans out, smiles and closes her eyes.

Soon she is aloft, borne away, no longer alone.

A Guttering of
Flickers

She's outside her father's room, a hand on the door, trying not to cry. Something's been forming inside of her, taking shape, building to a climax. Not the baby, something else. A choice. A resolution.

The baby.

Malcolm left when she told him. Didn't say a word. Gathered his things—and some of hers—and crept away in the night. He'd left one thing behind, she thought ruefully.

She looks at the closed door. Not many doors were ever open to her. And if they were, she never went through them.

Lizzie pushes through the door, into the room. Before dealing with her father, she goes into the side bathroom, looks in the mirror, rubs her red eyes, blows her nose. She stays in the bathroom a few minutes, breathing.

Her father is curled up on the rumpled bed. They'd caught him trying to open the window, fumbling at the latch. They told her he wanted to get some air; that she should visit. She knew it wasn't air he wanted.

Will he remember? She wonders if memories still reside in his head, dormant, waiting to be awakened. Memories of sunshine and holidays; loving, laughing and fucking.

The room smells of urine and Pine-Sol. Wan light oozes through a blind, spilling disease. She raises the blind. Grey light leeches into the room. Outside, perched in a tree, is a bird, small and black at the end of a thin branch, peering into the room. A Dark-Eyed Junco, she thinks.

Mum would have known.

Her Mum's favourites were the Flickers, Common or Northern. They'd congregate at the back end of their country property where it bordered the woodlands. They were woodpeckers, but they often fed on the ground, collecting ants and beetles. Or they'd walk up the trees, drumming their beaks along the softening bark. They would call out *ki ki ki ki.*

"A guttering of Flickers," Mum once told her. "That's what you call a group of them."

Birders were odd, she thought back then. A guttering of Flickers.

A murder of Crows. A siege of Bitterns. A cauldron of Raptors. An unkindness of Ravens. She recalls reading a short story by Douglas Clegg; 'A Madness of Starlings'. Madness. It was an apt term, she thought. Later she learned the correct term for a group of Starlings is murmuration.

As she turns away from the window there is a small thud. She looks back to see a faint blur against the glass—like the smudge of an insect on a car's windscreen—then a small dark shape, falling away. She hurries to the window and gazes down, but there's no sign of the bird, just a faint stain on the window.

She remembers another stain, another time.

The eggs were small, fragile; in a glass case under heat lamps in a corner of the classroom. Mrs. Irwin, their teacher, had found the abandoned nest in her yard. She warned the class that they might not hatch, that they might already be dead.

Each day Lizzie would stare at the nest, at the three tiny eggs, expectant. One morning, as she was watching, a crack appeared in one of the eggs. She could see the egg moving. She knew the baby inside was trying to get out. Soon, more cracks materialized, spreading along the egg like spidery veins. Then a small hole appeared, and a tiny yellow beak breached the shell. Soon after, a tiny hatchling emerged from the broken egg, all wet and pink and naked. The bird tottered and cried weakly, as did Lizzie.

They nursed the bird, kept it warm, fed it with an eyedropper. It was the only egg that hatched. The next morning Lizzie went in early to see the baby bird. She reached into the case, cradled the tiny thing, and pulled it from its nest. She cooed to the bird. It thrashed, startling Lizzie, and she dropped it. Panicked, she reached clumsily for the bird, and her knee came down hard on the tiny thing. There was a squishing sound, and a small whoosh like escaping breath. And when Lizzie lifted her leg, all that was left was a splayed red ruin and thin little bones.

On the bed a vague lumpy form stirs, breaking Lizzie from the reverie. He is bloated from the drugs. He opens sleep-caked eyes.

Sometimes she thinks she sees something in his fathomless eyes, in the way he cranes his head, almost bird-like, and peers at her unblinking. Faint recognition. Faint hope.

Something.

Sometimes.

"Mary?" the hazy form asks.

She forces a smile and steps forward, hesitant. She sits on the edge of the bed, places a hand on his cold leg. "No, Dad," she says. "Lizzie."

He's staring past her, at the window.

She gulps. "Your daughter."

"Mary?" Pleading.

"Mary is gone." A bright burst of anger stabs her. "Mary's dead."

His fever-eyes scurry like black ants on sun-scorched rocks. *"Mary."*

Another sound, like a faint cry, and she turns. There's another bird outside on the branch, looking in. She squints. A Pipit? Another Junco? It couldn't be the same one, could it? It would be dazed still. She crosses to the wide window, stares out. It's a Flicker, she now sees: spotted breast with a splash of red near its curved bill. The bird cocks its head, stares. When she was younger she thought it a plain bird. But it's really quite beautiful. She thinks of Mum. Inexplicably, her eyes film over with water.

Ki ki ki, she hears. She presses her nose to the glass and peeks down. There are dozens of the birds on the ground. Some are tottering along, thin bills poking rivulets into the earth to feed, but most are still and staring up at her.

Her stomach rolls.

A guttering.

There's a groan from the bed. Dad is trying to get up.

He's pushed the covers off, and his diaper has come loose. She wipes her eyes and rushes to the bed.

"Thirsty," he says, white-larval tongue licking his lips.

She pats his hand. He smiles faintly. His smile is as cold as his hand.

Lizzie grabs the pitcher from the bedside table. It's empty. She goes into the tiny bathroom and fills the pitcher with tepid water.

Someone has left a pair of bloodied scissors on the countertop. She blinks in confusion, pockets the scissors, and returns with the water. She pours a glass, holds it up to his parched lips. He sips at the water, then leans back, grinning.

She stares at his swollen body. It's the side effects of the experimental medication, they told her. Steroids. That was the way of the world, she thought. Keep throwing shit against the wall and hope some of it sticks. Keep trying different meds. Never mind the patient, he's an experiment now. Steroids, anti-amyloids, coagulants, atypical antipsychotics, inhibitors. Something's got to work. Doesn't it?

Evidently not.

His belly looked like hers now. Swelling. Pregnant.

"Mary," he says again.

This time she checks herself. Smiles. Lies. "Yes."

That placates him. He closes his eyes. Noises emanate from his mouth; gurgling, choking sounds. And something else. A strange murmuring.

Something stirs inside of her. In her gut. Only recently has she felt movement in there. It fills her with a queer dread. She'd thought, perhaps, nothing would move in there. Thought it might all be a bad dream.

But it is real.

And the thought of a living thing stirring in her, awakening, makes her queasy with fear. Would it break through, open her up, hatch like a bird?

There's a tapping, a thudding. It's the bird again, or another, flying against the window in a black blur, trying to get in. She grimaces. And there is her father—"We found him at the window, fumbling with the latch."—desperate to get out.

Thud thud. Tap. Thud tap.

A knocking, from outside. It's almost as if it's in her head, or her stomach.

Knock.

Like a stranger at your door at midnight. Someone wanting in. Something wanting out.

As a child, whenever there was a knock at her front door, she'd wonder who it was. Who is out there?

Instead of Brylcreemed salesmen selling vacuums or encyclopedias, she'd imagine a host of possibilities: a Harlequin with a trick deck of playing cards and a sly grin inviting her to a game of chance; an alien with large eyes like black ink asking her for directions to some distant world; an impish fairy on a sun-dappled forest path gesturing for her to follow along.

But she never answered those doors. Another opportunity lost.

Her father groans. Or perhaps it is her. She wonders what's inside her father. Wonders why they can't get it out.

Strange sounds and strange stirrings. Murmurations. A guttering. She can't tell if it is from her or the window or her father. It's from everywhere. Something is trying to breach this world. Or escape it.

It's inside of her. And her father. Desperate to get out.

She looks at her father, at his swelling belly, then to her own belly, back to her father, who is smiling, eyes wide and expectant.

Then the scissors are in her hands, and there's an ache inside of her. In her gut. There's always been an ache inside of her. Her eyes film over, blur, but she sees something like a talon or a beak poking from her stomach. Then it is out, on the floor, wet and trembling and crying for its mother.

Hungry, the Rain-God Awakens

Eyes wide,

you stir, wake from your ancient slumber—
coal-ash in your clotted throat, knife-twist hunger in your belly,
pain-twinge in your heart.

Arms wide,

you twirl in the oily menthol rain,
whirling dervish, dancing conjurer.
A downpour of bloated grey toads,
puddles of flopping, mouth-mewling Jesus fish,
a sidewalk of salamanders.

And you,

a trickster in this new mad world,
lick your thin parched lips.

Mouth wide,

head thrown back, you stand in the ropy rain
and fill your gullet with corpulent fish, squirming amphibians.
You crunch down with red razor-teeth, chew, swallow—
black juice running down your chin, and you

smile wide,

bird-song trilling in your throat, contentment brewing in your belly,
love blossoming in your primordial heart;
as you grin a razor-grin, and roam along
the blood-slick road,
in search of larger prey.

Conversations with the Dead

The dead boy crawls up out of the crevasse and settles beside me on the rocky outcropping.

"What's it like, Alex," I ask, "being dead?"

Alex looks at me with eyes like cold milk and smiles faintly. He sighs.

"Not so different," Alex says. He turns, gazes across the low valley toward the horizon and a scarlet-scudded sky.

"I don't sleep," Alex says. "Or eat. But I don't miss those things. I don't have a girlfriend, either. Never did." He trembles. "How can I miss something I never had?" He turns to me. "*You* have a girlfriend?" he asks.

"Yes," I lie.

He twists around, studies the skyline as if searching for something. He is ghost-still. Quiet. Conversations with the dead aren't so different from conversations with the living.

I'd met Alex the previous week. I was atop Hanlon's Point when Alex came crawling out of this impossibly thin fissure in the rock.

I leapt up. "What the...?"

Ragged Alex had stood. "Have you come for me?" he asked in a reedy voice.

I knew he was dead. He had that air of disquiet solitude. He didn't look much different than Grand Dad had in his silky coffin, only dirtier.

Alex tottered on the uneven ground, just another sad, skinny, dead kid.

Every day this summer, when I'd visit Hanlon's Point, he'd come crawling up out of that skinny wedge.

"Who?" Alex asks.

"What?" I say, puzzled.

"Your girlfriend? What's her name?"

I turn away. "You don't know her."

Alex sighs a ghostly sigh. Which is to say it sounds sadder and more forlorn than a regular sigh. A ghost sigh.

"Try me," he says.

I was a coward. I couldn't even tell the truth to a dead boy. I look down, toe the dirt with my sneaker. "Okay, I don't actually have a girlfriend. Not in the real sense."

Dead Alex grins. "Thought so. That's okay. It'll happen. And when it does I want you to tell me what it's like. Because I don't have one in the real sense, either. Never will."

"Sure," I say. "I'll tell you all about it. If you're still here."

Alex stares at me, unblinking, his face sad and sagging. Almost as sad as Mom's face. Hers is a face of cheerless gloom. The face of a mother who has lost a child.

I won't be dating any girls any time soon. I am tall and thin and gawky. Pimply-faced. I eat alone in the school cafeteria. I have never kissed a girl. I am deader than Alex.

Alex stares at me with his face full of hurt.

"Sorry," I mutter, standing. "I have to go." I trudge down the hill, not sparing a glance at my depressed ghost friend.

The dead kid is my only friend in this world.

Dinner is on the table. Lasagne, garlic bread, and salad. I sit.

Dad says, "You're late." Doesn't look up from his plate.

Mom looks at me, half smiles. "I haven't seen you much lately. Where are you going after school?"

"Hanlon's Point," I say. I fork pasta into my mouth even though I'm not hungry. "It's peaceful." I glance at dad, let my gaze linger. "No one there to bother me."

Mom says, "I wish you'd make friends."

I think of Alex, pale and alone. "I have a friend," I say. "Met him at Hanlon's Point."

This time dad does look up. "You gay?" he asks. He has pasta sauce on his face.

I chuckle, shake my head. Typical. "What do you think?" I ask.

Dad shovels food into his mouth, chews, shrugs his shoulders. "Who can tell?" he says. "You're so God damn… skinny."

His logic defeats me. I spear a noodle. "Would it help," I ask, "if I went up stairs right now with one of your magazines, the ones you keep in the garage?"

"Glendon!" Mom says. "Watch your tongue." She only calls me Glendon when she is angry with me.

"Yeah," Dad mumbles through a mouthful of bread. "It would."

I stand. "As you wish." I turn and start up the stairs.

"No, Glen," Mom says. I don't look back. I can picture her weaving about the small kitchen like a caged bird, her hands fluttering madly. "Don't," she says.

I go into my room, lie on my bed and do nothing. Dad will grunt and head to the garage for a secret cigarette. Mom will open and close the kitchen cupboards, and try not to think about what I might be doing up here. I smile at that. It is a small, cruel thing, but it is all I have.

I sit on a smooth section of the outcropping, near the crevasse. Alex slowly pulls himself out of the small crease in the stone. He doesn't look good. I guess, when you're dead, things start to go.

"Have you come for me?" Alex says.

"No," I answer, "it's just me."

"Oh," Alex says, disappointed.

"Is that your standard line?" I ask. "Who do you think is coming for you?"

Alex shrugs. "Dunno. Just a feeling that I'm not supposed to stay here. That this is temporary."

It is my turn to shrug. "Everything's temporary. Life and death." I shoot him an angry look. "I've news for you. I don't come up here for you. I do it for me. Besides, does anyone else ever come up here?"

Alex picks at a piece of rotted skin dangling from his cheek. "Sometimes. But no one else seems to notice me. It was like that in real life, too."

I chuckle mirthlessly, hug my knees to my chest. "We aren't so different, me and you," I say. "Other than you being dead, that is."

"How come you can see me, Glen?" Alex asks. "Haven't you wondered?"

I look at Alex, glance at his wrists. He folds his arms in, trying to hide the ragged scars, the vertical slashes, as if I hadn't seen them, as if, even now, dead, he is ashamed of all his wounds. We all have wounds, I guess. Some are more visible than others. He just stares at me, waits for an answer.

I look away. "In some ways, I guess, I'm as dead as you."

I'm in the baby's room, sitting in a wicker rocking chair, holding a stuffed teddy, staring at the empty crib. My near-brother's room.

The room is done in a tasteful pale blue, but it's stuffy and overly warm in here. Some of the paint on the walls has begun to crack and peel, reminding me of Robin's eggs, as if a chick were going to hatch from the wall. But nothing living will ever reside here.

It nearly broke my mother. She was six weeks from term when there were complications. The baby developed an infection and died suddenly. There were other medical complications, forcing mother to carry the baby to term. It was a sad day when she and father went to the hospital. It is a terrible weight to carry a dead baby thing inside of you.

I often come in here and visit the baby. More to the point, on occasion, he visits me.

I stare at the empty crib, cradle the stuffed bear, and wonder if dead-baby will make an appearance when I blink and he's there, small and bloody and mewling, on the crib's mattress. He's so small and so bloody, but still cute, like any baby.

The baby can't talk, of course, so our conversations are one-way affairs, like the conversations I have with dad. Sometimes I'll say something and dead-baby will start, kick his wee legs, pump his tiny fists (and have you ever noticed how babies' hands always curl into tiny fists, as if we're all born angry?) and roll toward me, mouth opening and closing, as if he's trying to speak, but the only thing that comes out is a strange choking sound. That's as good as our conversations get.

I rock back and forth in the chair. I fold my arms and imagine

I'm cradling the baby. The baby sleeps, content. Then my imaginary baby is a still and bloody thing, so I stop rocking, stand and approach the crib.

"I would have rocked you every day," I say. "Every night."

Dead-baby stares at me wide-eyed and unblinking. He gurgles, and blood-flecked drool oozes from his mouth. He's beautiful. I resist the urge to pick him up.

He grins, red and wide.

"You sure are cute," I say, because even dead babies need reassurance.

I go back to the rocking chair and start up again, back and forth. I wish dead-baby had been born. I would have liked a little brother.

Rock-a-bye baby, I think, and my eyes drift shut.

Alex kicks at a patch of ground, like any normal kid. Any normal dead kid. "I never even kissed a girl."

I am silent. I know Alex is baiting me. He is a tricky ghost.

"You?" Alex asks.

"Christ," I say, "you know I don't have a girlfriend, so what do you think?"

Alex stares, blinks, looks away. "Sorry," he mutters.

I hurt his feelings. Ghosts have feelings, too.

"It's okay," I say. "I understand."

Alex looks down, continues to scuff at the ground with his foot. "I don't have many people I can talk to." He gives me a sheepish ghost grin. "You're it."

"Maybe," I say, "we weren't meant to have girlfriends."

"What do you mean?" Alex says.

"Guys like us. Loners. Who would want us?"

Alex stares at me, a queasy expression crossing his face. I think he's going to cry. He turns, squints into the distance, into that forever sky. When he speaks, it is whisper soft.

"You're right, Glen," he says, turning back to me. "No one."

I look at Alex. I wonder what would happen if I reach out and touch him?

"Aren't there others like you?" I ask. "Can't you talk to them?"

"There's never been others like me," Alex says. He is quiet a moment, then adds, "If there were… I'd probably still be alive."

"You're so beautiful," I say. I'm in my room. I'm talking to my pillow. The pillow is propped up against the headboard. I'm practicing on the pillow. I might meet a girl one day. I might talk to her, ask her out. Maybe.

I look down, feigning embarrassment. "Sorry. That's awfully forward." I'm trying to sound adult, grown up, like all the kids in school rushing headlong into adolescence, as if age really does bring wisdom. If only they knew.

I look up. The pillow does not respond. It never does. Sometimes, though, I blink and the pillow isn't a pillow but is a girl, a brunette with wavy brown hair and green eyes. A girl with red lips and a warm smile; with freckles, even, and a tiny mole above her lips. Or a short cute blond girl with a pleasant attitude. It makes no difference. I don't have any particular fantasy girl. *Any* girl is my fantasy girl.

"It's okay," my pillow-girl says. "It's a compliment. Thank you." The pillow girl blushes, blinks, smiles. "You're cute."

"Th-Thank you," I pretend stammer. Then I lean in, stroke the pillow case and give it a long kiss. I think about moist lips and wet tongues. Soft skin. I grab the girl, kiss her, my mouth nipping, tongue exploring. And my pants are off. I'm on top of her, and I'm trying to go slow, but my movement becomes urgent, and she's under me, soft and warm and smiling, eyes rolling in pleasure, moaning, and then I release (too soon, I think) and lay there panting, gasping "I love you," and when I gaze up it's just a pillow, a sticky pillow, and it is just another conversation with a dead thing, and another day of laundry.

Dad is in a black mood. I can see it from down the block. See it in his body language. He's standing in front of the house, taut and coiled. Waiting.

School administrators have phoned, no doubt. I knew they would, eventually. I haven't been to class all week. I've been hanging out with Alex, or going to the music shop and checking out the CD's I can't afford. The public library, too. I can browse the stacks of books, spend hours reading pulp novels. Anywhere I can escape for a little while. Inevitably, though, you have to face things.

I consider stopping, turning around and walking away and never returning. That's how they do it in books and movies. Our stoic hero wandering off into the sunset, not a care in the world, never to return, his strength implicit in his decision.

Life isn't a Hollywood movie.

I slow my pace, take my time walking up to the house. It'll antagonize him further, I know, and I hate myself for inflicting these little cruelties.

"Where have you been?" he asks, his voice a low growl.

"Around," I say. "Just around."

He tenses, jaw clenching. "You haven't been at school."

I blink. "So?"

Now it's his turn to blink. He doesn't know how to answer that. He's incredulous. I can see it in his face. And he's angrier than I've ever seen him.

He looks left, then right, then straight at me. "So?" he says, with quiet malice.

We stare at each other, father and son, like mortal enemies.

He's red-faced, shuddering. "You're less than useless," he says.

"It's an inherited trait," I say.

Dad grins unpleasantly. "Son of a bitch," he says, his fist rising.

I flinch, close my eyes and wait, but the expected blow doesn't come. I open my eyes and he's standing there, shaking, fist in the air, gaping at me.

I quickly lean forward, and with both hands pull his face to mine and kiss him hard on the lips, holding him tight to me until he pulls away sputtering and falls to the ground.

Then, before he can get up and come at me, I sprint away, down the street, feeling neither particularly strong nor heroic.

Alex is waiting for me. "I knew you'd come," he says.

"How?" I ask.

He shrugs, smiles. "I know you. We're more alike than you think."

So I tell him what happened.

"What will you do?" Alex asks.

Up here, near the plateau, the wind is cool and biting. Today, it smells of damp regret.

"I haven't figured that out," I answer. "I might never figure it out."

Alex regards me with a look of sad concern. "You'll have to go back," he says. "Eventually."

"Yes," I say. "One day."

"Don't be like me," Alex says, a note of pleading creeping into his voice.

I chortle, but it isn't a very happy sound. "You said we were alike."

"We are," Alex says. He folds his hands, tries to hide them in his lap, cover his wounds. "All I mean is, don't be like me in *that* way."

"You needn't worry," I say.

"What was it like," Alex asks, "when you kissed your father? Why did you do it?"

"Because it was the cruellest thing I could think of."

I look at Alex, this dead boy with worry and sorrow etched in his features. I smile. For him and for me. Again I wonder, what would happen if I reach out and touch him? And instead of wondering, I lean in, and Alex leans in, and our lips touch, our mouths press together, and for a few precious seconds everything seems right, this sharing, this experience. It's something we both need.

Then, inside me, something shifts and settles, like a puzzle piece falling into place. And I open my eyes to an expansive grey sky, empty except for a lone crow on the horizon flying off into a single wedge of wan light. Alex is gone. As if he were never really there in the first place.

And it's just me, alone.

I keep returning to Hanlon's Point, but Alex never materializes. He's slipped away, finally, like a true ghost, as if that kiss was all he needed.

A kiss.

Some tenderness.

Companionship.

Some love.

It's all any of us really need.

Now it's my turn to wait, here in the dark, in the deep crevasse.

Waiting to crawl into the light.

The Beach

The lonesome beach. The shrieking gulls. The ceaseless rain.

Elspeth hears the rain, beating against the window in an incessant murmur. Rain is her religion now. Rain and the changing seasons. It's all she has left. It's all she believes in.

All too soon summer is over, she thinks. It's autumn now, the rainy season, and soon it will be winter. The seasons pass quickly. Elspeth sighs. The years pass quickly, too.

She moves to the front window. It's another grey day. For a moment all she can see is herself reflected back to her from the dark pane. She doesn't recognize the face. It's as if someone else, some other Elspeth, is outside on the damp lawn staring in at her impassively, as if there is another her, another world beyond the thin pane. And sometimes, alone in her house, staring out her window, she truly believes there is another world, a thin place of shadows and unreality.

She moves closer to the rain-streaked window, and as she does, one of the Elspeths disappears. Which one is the real me? she thinks.

The cottage is silent except for the rain and the beating of her heart. Outside, she hears a gull cry. She pictures its small red-lidded eyes, its curved yellow beak. Sometimes all she can hear is their shrieking.

There is a pot of stew simmering on the stove, its savoury tang hanging in the air. She's made too much stew—there's only her—but what she doesn't consume in a few days, she'll freeze. She takes her small comforts where she can.

Outside, the rain falls in a steady, soothing rhythm. It puddles on the green lawn, the cracked sidewalk, and bumpy grey road. It runs in the gutters.

On the street, a small child in yellow rain-gear is splashing through a puddle. Elspeth smiles. She can feel her heart beating in time to the rain. Watching the child play, something inside her flares briefly, a sweet pain. She hearkens back to her own childhood, when she still believed. Then she grew up. She wished she'd never grown up.

Elspeth stares out the window, eyes dry and unblinking. She'd imagined a different life, or different lives. She thought she'd marry, have children. Then she thought she'd travel, maybe actually go to China, for her father's sake and for herself. Go to Chile. She'd seen a documentary once about Rapa Nui, Easter Island, thousands of miles off the coast of Chile. Huge carved stone heads covered the island. They were a mystery. Because of their strange proportions and their geometry, everyone assumed they were just heads. But they weren't. They had bodies under the ground. They'd been buried up to their necks. Implacable stone faces peering out to the ocean. It always made her think of her father. She wished she could have gone to Easter Island or China.

The girl, Anna, is walking through puddles, kicking dead leaves, searching for frogs and looking for fat worms. Her mother had told her not to get soaked. "You're too old," she'd warned, "for playing in puddles." Anna hopes she'll never be too old to play in the rain. Still, she'd made sure to put on her mackintosh and galoshes. It wouldn't do to return wet. She would get a smack. Maybe two, to make up for not having a father.

Like Elspeth, the cottage is old and small. It hasn't changed. Even as a child, when the world seemed impossibly big, the cottage appeared small to Elspeth. That was its charm, she supposed. That, and the lonely beach that ran outside the back door. As a child she'd spend her weekends on the warm summer sand with her plastic bucket and shovel, digging, making sand castles and moats, dreaming of far-off places. Back then, peering out to the far horizon where water met sky, the effect was of a wide, carnivorous smile, a thin wedge of unreality that thrilled and scared her. The world was vast and cosmic. The cottage was small and insignificant. Still, she thinks, it's big enough for one, for her.

Elspeth watches the child, a girl, she thinks—what boy would wear yellow?—playing in the rain. It's late in the season for children. Most of the families have left. Most everyone was gone. And Elspeth... well, Elspeth is used to being alone.

Anna is whistling, poking at a worm with a stick, when the woman appears. The woman has a hood over her head, hiding her face in shadow, but Anna can see that the woman is smiling.

"Shouldn't you be gone?" the woman says, not unfriendly.

Anna straightens, blinks.

"Home, I mean," the woman says. "Away from here. Back to school."

Anna drops the stick, steps closer, squints up at the hooded woman. "We always come late, my Mum and I," she says. "It's cheaper."

Elspeth considers, looks up and down the grey, empty street. "You shouldn't be out here," she says.

"I'm allowed," Anna says. "I like the rain. I'm going to be a meteorologist. Or a pilot."

Elspeth barks a laugh. The sound startles her. She can't recall the last time she laughed aloud. Perhaps there is hope for her yet. Perhaps she can reclaim some faith.

The rain is fat and unremitting. It streaks off Elspeth's rain hood and blurs her vision, as if she's crying. Overhead a gull cries, a white speck against the crumpled, dark sky. Elspeth shivers. "Would you like some lunch?" she asks. "Some stew?"

Her father ran away. Years later, her mother died. All she has left is the cottage and her memories.

Elspeth remembers the last weekend she'd spent with her father at the cottage before he left for good. They were on the beach. It was a sunny, cloudless day; blue skies and green water. The cool, salty breeze. The cry of gulls. He'd asked her if she wanted to dig to China.

"Let's see if we can dig to the other side of the world," her father said. And they tried.

Her father retrieved a shovel from the bed of his pick-up truck. They took turns digging the hole, laughing in the August sun. After a time, exhausted but happy, Elspeth stopped. "We'll never make it," she said, feigning disappointment.

Her father smiled, picked her up and placed her in the hole. Elspeth squirmed, kicked her legs, laughed. "We'll bury you," he said. "Just to your neck. Promise." And he began to fill in the hole. Elspeth was in the damp hole, buried to her neck. "Look at you," her father said. "From a distance, you could be a discarded beach ball. We best make sure no one tries to kick you." He smiled. "Hmmm, perhaps I'll go in for a bit, leave you to the gulls. Bye, El," her father said, turning.

"Dad, no!"

Her father turned back. "El, I'm joking. You know that." He dug her out of the hole, hugged her tight, kissed her forehead. "I would never leave you."

But he did leave her. A child shouldn't grow up without a father, she thinks. A child should never grow up.

"Is it good?" Elspeth asks the girl.

Anna looks up from the bowl of stew. "Yes. Delicious. My Mum doesn't cook. Not like this. Her specialty is grilled cheese. Heck, even I can make grilled cheese. But I like grilled cheese."

"And your father?" Elspeth asks.

Anna blinks, spoons stew into her mouth, swallows. "Don't know," she says. "Mum says he got scared. Took off." She rests the spoon in the bowl. "It's okay. I don't mind. My Mum tries."

Elspeth turns to Anna. "Would you like to go to the beach?" Then, "Would you like to go to China?"

"When I'm a pilot," Anna says, "I'm going to travel the world. When I'm grown up."

"I hope you never grow up," Elspeth whispers.

Anna brushes a strand of wet hair away from her eyes, squints at Elspeth, then looks toward the door.

Elspeth stares at the young, skinny thing. "Are you strong, Anna? Can you dig? Will you help me?"

"I have to go now," Anna says.

Once, long ago, when she was a young woman who still had faith in the world, there was a boy, Matthew. She'd met him on holiday, here at the cottage. He was on the beach, alone, tall and tan, blond and bright-eyed. On the beach, at night, he kissed her. And she believed in the power of love. Then, like summer itself, it ended.

"It's been fun," Matthew said, smiling, idly kicking the sand, "but I have to go now."

It was a grey day. The wind howled, and the gulls squawked. The beach was barren save for the two of them. The sand was a gritty irritant. It blew in Elspeth's face and brought tears to her eyes. She blinked, squeezed Matthew's hand. "You'll visit, keep in touch?" She hated the pleading tone in her voice.

Matthew shrugged his shoulders, released Elspeth's hand. "It was just a summer fling. Nothing more."

"Please," she said, "don't go."

"You need to grow up, El," he said. "I have to go now."

Then he was gone.

Elspeth stood alone on the dark beach with the wind and the gulls. Dark clouds filled the sky. Then it rained. Still she stood in the cold rain, unblinking, unmoving, staring at nothing. Alone.

It's raining, a pounding against the glass like gull wings. Elspeth moves to the back window. The beach is a thin dark finger of soft bone. Rain blurs the windowpane, and for a moment all she can see is herself reflected back to her from the dirty glass. She doesn't recognize her face. It's as if some other Elspeth is out there on the dark sand staring in at her.

She moves closer and one of the Elspeths disappears. She leans against the cool glass, squints.

She sees a pale world like stretched canvas, a thin veil, grey and unending, no line on the horizon.

She sees the water, dark and rumpled muslin, heaving.

She sees the wet black sand, a dark round shape, and the shrieking, hungry gulls.

The long, empty beach.

The ceaseless rain.

Down the Rabbit Hole

Quiet in the car. Sheila glances at her watch. The second hand moves listlessly like the traffic, like her heart, as if the universe were winding down.

Tick.

Time is running out.

She puts a CD into the player. She hopes it'll break the black tension.

Brad grimaces. "Tori Fuckin' Amos."

She'd suggested a cottage—a porch; the call of loons; slow sex. She missed the sex, whether slow or rushed. She hoped to rekindle that flame.

Sheila knew about his dalliances: working late; secretive phone calls. It was as if her heart had been punched out, leaving a black hole as indifferent as the cosmos. She'd get her heart back.

They'd been inching along the highway, Brad's mood growing blacker. Sheila looks at him—rigid, death-grip on the wheel, staring straight ahead—and exhales a breath she hadn't known she'd been holding. It's too late. This was a mistake. She's lost him down some rabbit hole. Sheila weeps.

Brad yanks the wheel to the right, speeds up the emergency lane and pulls off at the nearest exit. A dust-strewn road.

Sheila stumbles from the car, shuffles away. Her ankle twists. She falls. There's a dark hole in the ground like an unblinking eye. She leans over the hole. Cold, ancient air strokes her face. Instinctively, she reaches over, pulls on the edges. It yawns wider.

Brad looms above her. "A mistake," he affirms.

She points. "Look."

Brad scrunches down, leans forward. "Huh?"

Sheila shoves, and Brad tumbles down the hole. She pushes on the edges. The hole closes greedily, like a mouth. Sheila rolls over, stares up at the darkening sky.

There's your Tori Fuckin' Amos, she thinks. Her heart moves like a fresh-wound timepiece.

Tick.

These White Sorrows

He must be dreaming.

It's cold. So cold that the maple and birch trees are cracking. *Crack!* And then another crack. Like a gunshot.

Martin can't breathe, he's suffocating. The room is freezing and his lungs are full of ice. He wakes, bolts upright from the bed, gasping. Instinctively, he looks to the empty place on the bed beside him. Gillian. He'd been dreaming of her again.

Martin hears a whimper, a small cry. He must be dreaming.

Martin is in the chair by the window, his cold, shaking hands fumbling at the radio dial, trying for a signal, hoping for some news, any news. But the radio is nothing but white noise and black static. He peers through the ice-glazed glass at a world sheened in brittle, glittering frost-white. Beside him on the small table there is a cup of weak herbal tea the colour of pale, pinkish blood. Martin is cold, he is lonely. He aches. He believes he may crack like the frozen trees.

Winter, Martin thinks, is a season of white sorrows. With Gillian, winter was bearable, enjoyable even. Now it left him sluggish and in a stasis. He would cry if he could, but even the small benefit of melancholia has deserted him.

Yesterday, when Martin had gone out to the shed for firewood, he'd seen Gillian again. She was out on the frozen pond, silent and staring back at him. He knew it was her—*who else would it be?* he thought, grimly—she was still wearing that ugly red coat that Martin hated. The firewood slipped from his shaking hands. He picked up the shotgun. Martin closed his eyes and counted slowly to ten. Once he opened his eyes, she'd be gone, he hoped. It worked that way in reality. The grieving mind played tricks. Except she wasn't gone, and this wasn't reality. He opened his eyes and she was still on the ice, as he knew she would be. The wind caught her hair, whipped it around. Ice and snow whirled on the frozen surface of the pond, cocooning her. She resembled an icy Medusa. His beautiful Gillian, an ice maiden. Martin was suddenly scared to look at her, lest he turn to frozen stone. He looked away, and when he finally gathered the courage to turn back, she *was* gone. Vanished. As if she'd never been there.

He didn't think his heart could crack any more.

He'd gathered up the shotgun and firewood and gone back to the house. There'd been a set of fresh boot prints near the house, and he went rigid with fear and heartache. He went inside, locked up, and checked every room, especially the side room, just to be certain, then sighed in relief. He grimaced, shook his head. *Sleep*, he thought, *I need some rest.*

But sleep was no balm. He'd often see her in his dreams, his nightmares. And it was at night, when it was coldest, that he could hear the trees cracking like gunfire, their sap freezing, their bark splitting. He'd be in his bed, in the winter-dark room, shaking from the cold, and he'd hear a loud *crack!* Like a gunshot. *Exactly* like a gunshot. Only he knew it was the trees cracking. Just the trees. He'd wait awhile, listening for another loud retort, and just as he would begin to think it was over, just as he was finally settling back to sleep, another bang would sound, louder than the first, and he'd be jarred back awake. It always sounded so close. As if it was in the next room, the side room. He thought he could hear her out there, as well, shuffling through the snow, slinking and sniffing around the doors and windows. And he tried to pay no heed to the small cries and whimpers. So, he'd slept fitfully, if at all, ever since Gillian had gone.

Gone.

He chuckles mirthlessly at that. Gone. As if she had just gone into town for supplies and was coming back.

As if.

Martin blinks, hitches his breath, and rubs dry eyes. He is trembling. He lifts the chipped teacup and sips the cooling liquid. It is bitter. *He* is bitter. He rubs his arms for warmth. If you let it, the cold could get to you. It had gotten to Gillian.

The city had gotten to Martin.

One morning on the train it got to be too much for Martin. The drear and monotonous routine—wake, eat, shower, commute, work, eat, work, commute, eat, sleep—wore him down. The walking dead.

He'd been doing it for more than twenty years. It was city living, but it wasn't any kind of *life*. He'd got off the train and immediately took the next one back home. He didn't even call in sick. Turned off his cell phone. He stayed at home the rest of the week sleeping, reading books he'd always wanted to read, watching films he'd always wanted to see, walking, getting out and breathing the air and feeling the sun shining on him, or the rain rolling off his skin. A cleansing. A detox. A rebirth.

It was a revelation.

Gillian was apprehensive. She'd had a good job, a few friends. Some roots in the city. *A family*, she'd said. *We were going to start a family.*

He'd smiled, stroked her cheek, brushed the hair from her forehead. *Yes*, he said. *We can. We will.*

So, she did it for him. She'd done everything for him. They sold their house, took their savings and moved north, to a place of trees and lakes, ice and snow, bears, foxes, deer, and wolves. Yes, for him.

What had he ever done for her?

Nothing. He couldn't even put a bullet in her head.

He was blind, selfish. He couldn't see her unhappiness. Didn't want to see it.

It's coming for me, Martin. For us.

It was the illness talking, he knew. He'd tried to reassure her. *There's nothing out there, Gillian. There's nothing coming for us.*

Yes, there is. The cold. She went silent. Then, quietly, as if afraid to rouse something, *I can feel it.*

Martin blinks. He remembers the sound of her voice. An icy, exhausted susurration. Martin trembles. The house is cold, always cold, no matter how often he stokes the fire. He can feel it, deep inside his bones, a brittle chill spreading.

He blinks again as something passes by the window. A blurry smudge of red, like a streak of blood across a frozen grey sky. *Gillian?* He tenses. The shotgun is a few feet away, always close. The door is bolted, though, and the windows locked and frozen in place. He's safe, for now. Safer here, at any rate, than in the cities. The cities are overrun. Soon, he thinks, even this desolate icy wasteland will succumb. After all, we all eventually yield to our very existence. He blinks, shivers, and there are fresh, wet tears in his eyes.

Martin rises unsteadily, stumbles to the sink and rinses out the teacup. He grabs the shotgun, goes into the bedroom and lies down. He dozes and dreams. And his dreams are filled with the din of trees cracking and shotguns firing. Filled with cries and moans, feral and insistent.

Martin taught her how to ski and snowshoe. They had a snowmobile, and a pick-up truck for seasonal trips into Foleyet or Cochrane, but the woods were best traversed by skis or snowshoe. They would set out just after a fresh snowfall. They'd made paths through the trees. The skis would glide along the new blanket of snow *swish swish*. The snowshoes made a satisfying crunch. At first, it seemed the woods were silent, but as they grew accustomed to their surroundings they began to hear, to experience, the woods; the peculiar lament of the winter wind; the scuttling, burrowing sounds of rabbits and foxes; the shadow of an eagle (and sometimes its shrill cry) passing above in the clear, expansive sky; the sense that something watched them from a distance, among the trees. Martin thought that he could even *smell* the bears and wolves when they were close by. And later, while Martin and Gillian lay tangled up in each other for baby-making, for warmth, comfort, and security, the trees cried out, cracking and snapping like ancient dry bones.

Martin stirs, opens his dry eyes. Morning. Quiet. Hazy crepuscular winter light leaks into the room. His head hurts. Did he sleep? The snapping winter trees didn't wake him. Silent. Too silent. But his brain is a frozen fog, a swirl of icy torment. His body trembles with more than the cold. It's coming for him now, he knows. There's something he needs to do, though. Something important before it takes him. For his family. But his thoughts are a jumble of sharp shards and he's powerless as his eyes close, leaving him in darkness.

He must be dreaming. But his eyes are open to the same diffuse, translucent light. Did he sleep? He blinks as a reddish smear occludes the light from the frozen window. He's shaking and his head is a jangle of static, buzzing. Under the fuzzy interference the room and the world are still, quiet. Too still.

Martin rises slowly and grabs the shotgun from the side of the bed. It's time, he thinks. Finally. It's come for him and he can't put it off any more.

He moves to the side room, opens the door and steps in. The same weak light. He blinks wetly, tears running down his face. And outside he can now hear a faint shuffling, and a sniffling, as if from an animal.

He turns to the corner of the room and ambles over to the small bed. She's on the bed, his little girl. *Their* little girl. His heart thumps. He's vibrating, crying. His daughter looking up at him. Staring and grinning, unblinking. Stirring, as if roused from some ancient slumber.

Unsteadily Martin raises the shotgun. Somewhere he thinks he hears the crack and cry of a frozen tree, a frozen heart.

He must be dreaming.

This Red Night

Some nights the sky pulsed red, like a heart. Hearts could break, she knew, fill and burst. A crimson aurora.

On this red night, she stood outside the cabin, the shrieking north wind cutting ruts in the snow, in her flesh, stinging; eyes watering crystalline tears like diamonds. And the dogs... the dogs howled, paced. She spoke to them, assured them, steadied them with strong hands, and stronger words, because words, the right ones, were something she knew well.

Inside her, something stirred. She turned to the sky, a garnet-black canvas, leaking. She squinted. There was a churning, inside her. It was coming. Something wondrous. Something awful.

The red sky dripped, painted the frozen world, spatters of arterial-red on arctic-white. Blood on a page.

She stood with the pack, staring into the red night, unblinking, unmoving, waiting for something terrible, something lovely.

After a time, the sky settled. Red to indigo to tar-black. Stars like spotted jewels winking alien intelligence. The lamentable winter wind ceased shrieking. The dogs rested. She went inside. Sat at the keyboard. Waited. Stared at the screen. Pixels. Black and white like the numinous night. She listened. White noise, black static. Snow and ice and wind. She closed her eyes, saw red and black, bloody and corpse-stiff. Saw treeless hills, rocky ice-rimmed ridges, an empty outpost. She saw a crevasse, deep and dark, exquisite pain, a wound in the earth. She heard creatures crashing through the brush, something baying, and a slowly increasing thump. Thump.

It began. *Thump... thump.* The great machine. *Thump-thump.* An ancient beast awakening.

The wind cried, and the dogs moaned. The cabin shook. The ground thrummed, and the very earth vibrated.

It was coming, as it always did, as it always would. Something terrible, something lovely.

And the sky filled crimson again, like a heart filled to bursting with love and pain, as all hearts are. Then it broke, again—as it always did, as it always would—shards of redness splintering. Hard ruby-chips piercing like arrows. This red night. This red anguish.

Sky and snow. Red and white.

Then she began, fingers punching out letters, words, fiction, truth.

Writing. Red and black and white. Sky and snow. Truth and fiction. Writing. Aurora-red, arctic-white, borealis-black. Nothing but sky and snow. More blood on the world's infinite page.

And the great, hungry machine awakening. *Thump thump.*

Pieces of Blackness

He watched the night sky. It was black and alien, churning darkly, expanding, living and growing, like the pain that coursed through him. He watched and waited. It was a dark sky, but he could see another darkness, pieces of tainted blackness, tumours, coiling, forming a greater blackness. One day, he knew, it would open up, all of it; the sky, him, and the entire world.

Every time he watched the sky, he was reminded of the boy.

Peter never told anyone about the boy. He kept it all inside of him, a cancerous darkness, pieces of a blacker blackness, living and growing. He could taste it, a rancid foulness, a murky mass twisting inside him, expanding and solidifying, like black stones tumbling and pulverizing his insides, a dark pain that doubled him over and made Peter vomit gobs of brown mucous.

But Peter never told anyone about the pain, or the pieces of blackness living inside of him.

"Come back. Please, come back."

"Peter. Peter? Wake up."

Peter moaned, rolled over. He was dreaming. It wasn't one of his dark nightmares. This was a proper sex dream: soft lips kissing, long booted legs wrapped around him, limbs twining, groping, gloved hands stroking.

Those hands were rough now, shoving, shaking.

"Peter! Wake up!"

He groaned, pushed the dream away and sat up, blinking. Katy was staring at him, one hand clutching his arm. "You okay?" she asked.

An erection pushed against his boxers. Guilt niggled at him. He rubbed sleep from his eyes. "Yeah, sure, I'm fine. What time is it?" He glanced at the digital clock. 3:12.

"It's Timothy," Katy said.

Peter was suddenly wide awake. "What," he said. "What is it?"

"I heard something," she said.

Timothy was their son. He was six years old. Lately, he'd taken to sleepwalking. They'd woken one night to strange sounds from outside, to find Timothy in their barn, chuckling madly. The sight of their son in Winnie-the-Pooh pyjamas standing in the old, empty barn, laughing, had sent them reeling. It'd sent a dark spasm through Peter. *The barn*, he'd thought, *not the fucking barn.*

The adoption agency had explained that it takes quite an adjustment for young children to go from foster care to an adoptive family. Their family doctor surmised it was just a formative stage that Timothy would soon outgrow.

But he didn't. Two or three times each week they'd find Timothy in the bathroom or kitchen or garage, staring blank-eyed, face strained red, mouth agape in a grin of terror, guttural laughter coming from him. It'd take a while, but they'd comfort and soothe him with quiet whispers and soft touches until he'd seemingly snap out of it, or "wake up," then go back to bed as if nothing happened.

As if he didn't have a care in the world.

They put safety latches high up on the main doors, to prevent Timothy from getting out of the house. Peter had also wanted to lock Timothy's bedroom door, but Katy would have none of it. "He's not a fucking animal, Peter, a pet. He's a scared little boy. *My* little boy." It seemed to Peter that when it came to Timothy, he didn't have much say.

They'd compromised and put a baby monitor in his room, so they'd hear Timothy if he stirred. Peter hated it. Each night it hissed and crackled black static. He listened now, but could only hear that dread crackle like a television channel that's gone off air.

"I don't hear him," Peter said.

"*I* did," Katy said, sharp, and even in the near dark Peter could see her glower.

Peter stood, penis still half-erect, like something half-alive or half-dead. "I'll check on him," he said. He put on his robe and padded to the door.

The hallway was dark. Timothy's room was at the end of the hallway, as was the light switch. He took a step but a sound stopped him dead. It had sounded like a squeal, the kind of noise a mouse might make if you stomped on it. Then another sound, like a sigh, only breathier. Then that strange squeal again and he recognized it for what it was—a child's laughter, a strangled chuckle—and it sent a shiver through him.

"Timothy?" he called out. "Tim?"

In the darkness at the end of the hallway he sensed movement. A step forward. "Tim?"

Then a shadow, a piece of blackness, stirred, seemed to peel away from the far wall, and slipped into Timothy's room.

Peter raced down the hall. He flailed at the wall, trying to find the damn switch, but couldn't. He rushed into Timothy's room, found his switch and flipped it on. The sudden light hurt his eyes and made him squint. Timothy was sitting in his bed, cross-legged, body rigid, rocking, and smiling—no, Peter thought—grinning, as if a peculiar madness had taken hold. The same lunatic madness and dread that Peter now felt.

But as Peter moved toward the bed, Timothy seemed to sense his presence and looked toward him. Timothy blinked. His body relaxed. Then he lay down and closed his eyes, face calm, chest rising and falling in a natural rhythm.

Peter moved to the bed, stood staring at Timothy, his son. *Son.* He wondered, on nights like this, if he would ever truly think of the boy as *his* son. Wondered if he could be a father.

When Peter turned there was a shadow in the doorway: Katy. There was something a bit unnatural about her stance. She appeared to droop, sag, as if unseen hands or strings were holding her up.

Peter tried a smile. "It's okay," he said. "Everything is fine." And even as he said it, he didn't believe it.

Katy turned out the light, and then moved out of the doorway. When Peter followed and made it back to their bed, Katy had already seemingly fallen asleep. He had the sense that he'd done something. Or hadn't done something, as the case might be. He pulled the covers up and turned over. Somehow, he was still aroused. Peter tried to recall the last time he and Katy had sex. Not since Timothy had arrived, he realized.

The boy scared him.

The barn was old. It had been on the property for decades. The house, Peter's boyhood home, had been rebuilt twice during that time. Peter liked the barn. Katy didn't.

He stood in a far corner of the barn, smoking. Peter came out here to think. He came out here *not* to think. Katy would be displeased if she caught him smoking. So he kept watch on the barn door. She'd made him quit when they brought Timothy home. She didn't want him to be a bad influence. Peter smirked. Funny, he thought, Katy hadn't once mentioned Peter's health.

Peter finished the cigarette, stamped it out and pushed it into the corner. He closed the magazine, put it back in the box, covered it and shoved it behind a hay bale. Then he went back to the house.

Inside, Timothy was at the kitchen table, colouring in his Winnie-the-Pooh book. He loved Winnie-the-Pooh, especially Eeyore. Timothy reminded Peter of Eeyore; lonely, quiet, and sad.

Katy was at the counter chopping carrots, onion, and celery. Neither she nor Timothy had so much as glanced at Peter when he entered the kitchen.

"Where were you?" Katy said, not looking up.

"In the barn."

Katy stopped chopping. She looked up. "You're always out there, Peter. What do you get up to in that old place?"

Again, like recent days, guilt pulled at him. "Not much," he said. "Just checking for loose or rotted boards." He didn't know why he couldn't just tell her that he hadn't quit smoking. Maybe he didn't want to disappoint her any more than he already had. Didn't want her to see him as a failure.

You are *a failure*, part of him whispered.

Suddenly, Peter felt on the verge of tears.

"Are you okay?" Katy asked. "You don't look well."

Peter swallowed hard, pushed the emotion down. "F-fine," he said. "Perfectly." He tried to lighten the mood. "How's Timothy?" he said, and went to tousle the boy's hair, but Timothy shrank away from him.

Katy and Timothy were staring at him. Silent. Peter waved meekly. "I'll just go wash up," he said. Then he turned and left.

Pieces of blackness stirred in him, heavy. He'd been in pain, suffering, for a very long time. Ever since…

The boy scared him. He collected things in jars, the boy did. Dead things. Bugs, snakes, frogs. Timothy would take a large Mason jar and go out to the marshy area behind the house, hunting. When Peter saw the cricket in that first jar, he'd smiled, remembering his own youth. Days later the cricket was dead. Timothy hadn't punched any holes in the jar lid. So he'd shown him what to do; put some breathing holes in the lid, added grass and ants for food. Later, Peter noticed another jar on Timothy's dresser. It contained a dead Monarch butterfly, nothing else. There'd been no attempt to add food or breathing holes. "Timothy," he'd said. "You can't do that. You can't kill things."

Timothy had stared at him, unblinking. "Why not?" he'd said.

He had no good answer for that.

Children, Peter realized. That was the cause of their great strain.

Katy had always wanted children. When they had first started dating, Katy made those feelings known. They'd be out and she'd point to couples with a child, and remark about how happy they seemed. To Peter, those couples didn't appear any happier than any other people. They seemed regular, shuffling about, trying to get by, trying to make sense of things.

Before Katy, Peter hadn't really thought about children. When she broached the subject, he was noncommittal. But she pressed him, and though she never quite came out and said it, he felt she was making him choose. So he acquiesced, said he'd be happy to have children with her.

But they couldn't. Oh, they tried. He liked trying. They tried every conceivable method. To no avail.

So they were tested. And Peter was found lacking. Low sperm count. Peter remembered the disappointment registering on Katy's face: anger, sadness, regret, defeat. He *was* a failure.

Katy wouldn't be dissuaded, though. She wanted a child. So she needed sperm. But the thought of another man's sperm inside of Katy was too much for Peter. He knew it was irrational, but he couldn't get past it. All he could picture was another man fucking his wife, fucking her hard, and Katy enjoying it. He was being childish and petty but he couldn't reconcile those emotions.

They'd fought over it. Their first real fight. "We'll get a dog," Peter said. And Katy had laughed unpleasantly. "A dog? I want a child, a girl or boy to share our life, not a pet. I don't want something disposable. I want something permanent."

Nothing was permanent, Peter knew.

He surprised himself, though, by saying "We'll adopt. We will. It'll be good. We'll give someone a chance. A new life."

Katy brightened immediately, and warmed to the idea. She wiped tears from her eyes. "Really?" she said. "You sure?"

In fact, he wasn't sure, but he said it anyway. "Yes."

The boy scared him. He couldn't exactly explain why. Maybe it was the way he would stare at Peter, blank-faced and unblinking. Maybe it was the sudden short bursts of nervous laughter that would erupt from Timothy's mouth, and then die just as quickly, as if he'd been switched off. As if he wasn't a real boy but some automaton.

Peter stepped into the room, stared at the boy. Timothy was on his bed, a Winnie-the-Pooh book spread open on his lap. Peter glanced at the rows of killing jars on the boy's dresser. There was a large, fat bullfrog squeezed into one, its throat puffing in and out, eyes unblinking. It'd be dead in a few days, eyes still unblinking.

He couldn't bring himself to sit with the boy and read to him, play with him.

Or be a proper father, he thought.

Timothy looked up at him, and Peter shuddered and turned away.

Pain pressed at Peter's temples. He hadn't been sleeping well. No pornographic fantasy playing in his head. The hiss of the monitor beside his bed kept him awake at night. Beneath the constant static he thought he heard something else, the terrible childish chortle he'd heard in the hallway. A cruel, mocking laughter that Peter knew all too well.

Peter left the room and went down the hallway to the bathroom for some Advil. From the tiny window he could see their property. The field, the barn. Peter had many memories of the barn. Memories, he knew, were dangerous things.

The pain in his head pulsed. Peter closed his eyes seeking comfort in darkness, but black thoughts and distant memories churned in his head like thick mud. Bright pain cascaded across his dark vision. He smelled hay and sawdust; rotted wood and dry earth.

No!

Then a noise that made his ears prickle. Quiet laughter.

Come back.

Peter sensed something behind him. He opened his eyes and turned around. The boy was in the doorway, laughing mirthlessly. Peter shivered. His stomach flared in agony. He doubled over, retched, spewed dark brown liquid onto the floor. When Peter stood upright, the doorway was empty.

He stumbled to the sink cabinet, dry-swallowed a handful of Advil, and then staggered to his bedroom. Peter shut the door and closed the blinds. His body convulsed. His stomach heaved and more dark liquid spilled onto the floor. Then something *foreign* passed through him, a hard knot, and he retched again and a marble-sized object landed on the wet floor, dark and glistening, a piece of blackness.

The thrum of dark laughter made him reel. Peter covered his ears with trembling hands. His stomach churned, and his head buzzed, and the dark sky roiled, forming its greater blackness.

Peter was at that strange cusp, that dream-state between sleep and wakefulness, that grey purgatory.

He rolled over, felt Katy's body beside him, warm and lithe and smooth. He pressed into her, gentle, but insistent, almost desperate. She pushed back against him, the curve of her ass riding up against his cock. Peter moaned. Maybe he was dreaming. Maybe Katy was dreaming, too. He wondered what she dreamt, what she fantasized. Did she dream of fucking someone else? Two guys at once? A girl?

These fantasies spurred Peter. He pressed in tight against Katy, cupped a breast. She bucked against him. Someone moaned. The monitor crackled.

Peter pulled his pyjamas down, then yanked Katy's underwear aside and pushed into her. He grabbed her breast again, then held on, squeezed.

"Oh," Katy moaned.

Peter thrust and squeezed.

"Ow."

He felt moisture, pulled his hand away.

"Fuck," Katy said.

Peter struggled out of that grey purgatory and came awake. "W-What?" he said.

Katy sat up, turned on the lamp. Her white-cotton top clung to her breast, where a damp spot could be seen.

She lifted her top, examined the breast. Peter looked at his wet hand, wiped it on the bed sheet.

"What's wrong?" he said. "What is it?"

Katy looked at him quizzically. "It's milk," she said. "Breast milk."

The barn was quiet, secluded. Always had been. As a young boy, it was where he sought sanctuary, where he went to indulge in boyhood antics.

Quiet now. No hissing monitor. No laughing boy. No angry wife.

"You bastard," she'd hissed. "I'm not pregnant." She'd stared at him with something like pity. "I haven't been sleeping around." Then she'd cried, really cried, great sobs shaking her. Peter had just stood and stared. There'd been a time when he would have gone to her, put his arms around her, comforted her.

Their doctor admitted that, yes, it was a bit unusual for Katy to be lactating, but he'd heard of similar cases developing when a young child enters a household. The body reacts instinctively to nurture the new arrival.

Peter was now relegated to the living-room couch. At least he didn't have to listen to that black noise crackling from the baby monitor. Most days in the house he felt isolated and alone, like a specimen in Timothy's killing jars gasping for breath.

He took a long last draw on his cigarette, then stamped it out and hid the butt in the corner with the others. He rooted around behind a bale of old hay and pulled out the plastic milk crate covered in burlap. He drew a magazine from the crate; *Bitches in Bondage*. On the cover was a pale redheaded woman of indeterminate age, dressed in latex, on her knees, mouth gagged, and hands bound. Her eyes were wide and staring. At him. Peter thought, perhaps, that behind the gag she was smiling. At him.

Peter stepped behind the bale with the magazine. He loosened his belt, let his pants drop. He flipped through the pages. There was a buzzing in his head. Something was rising up within him, a black force that was great and alien and transcendent, churning. It would tear him apart.

The boy scared him.

Night. Peter shifted on the couch. He thought he'd heard something; the padding of tiny feet creaking across the upstairs hallway. And something else, as if from a dream or some distant recollection. A moan, laughter, echoing through the house and through his memories.

Peter stirred, sat up, listened. He thought he could hear the static and the hiss of the monitor, black interference, like the buzzing in his head. He stood. His body was taut and vibrating, like a plucked guitar string.

Another slow creak from upstairs. The boy was up and wandering again.

He blinked, rubbed his eyes, and headed for the stairs. It was dark-dark, like patches of blackness placed over other pieces of blackness. Somewhere a child was laughing quietly, he was sure of it. Peter crept slowly up the stairs.

Peter tottered forward. Black static filled the air. His head thrummed. He put a hand on the door, pushed it open, peered in.

Katy was on the bed, glassy-eyed, a small smile creasing her face, her shirt pushed up, exposing her breasts. The boy was sitting cradled in her lap, his mouth affixed to a breast, sucking. Katy moaned.

Peter quivered, let out a strangled sob.

Katy looked up, cheerlessly, stared at Peter unblinking. The boy suckled greedily.

"K-Katy," Peter croaked. He felt apart from reality, but rooted to the floor.

"It's okay," Katy said. "It's natural."

"But... no...."

"He's just a little boy," Katy continued. "My little boy."

Peter's stomach knotted. He wanted to rush over, pull the little vampire away from Katy, but the thought of touching the creature sent an icy black wave of repulsion through him. So he stood rooted and helpless. Always helpless.

The boy had stopped feeding. Both of them were looking at Peter now. Both smiling. The boy squinted, pointed, then laughed quietly. "I know you," the boy said.

Peter's hands flew up, as if he were trying to ward off something. He cried weakly, turned and ran from the room. He scampered down the hallway, down the stairs, through the front door and out into the night.

He thought he heard a voice, perhaps Katy's, perhaps his own, perhaps the boy's, saying *Come back come back*.

Electric pain coursed through him. Peter stopped, doubled over, and vomited dark stones and darker memories.

The boy scared him. Startled, Pete dropped the magazine. He quickly pulled his pants up, turned.

The boy backed away.

"No, wait," Pete said. His heart raced. He held out a hand.

The boy blinked, took another step back.

"It's okay," Pete pleaded. "Really." A piece of blackness coiled in his stomach, snaked through him, moved across his forehead, his vision. He moved forward.

"Petey," the boy said. "No."

Pete rubbed his eyes. It was like long fingers were digging into his brain, probing. He blinked. He thought he recognized the boy from school. He was a grade behind Pete.

The boy opened his mouth and laughed and laughed, mocking, and Pete's head burst in sharp black anguish.

He leaped. The boy gave a little yelp, and Pete pushed him to the ground, hard, and the boy went still. Pete lay on top of the boy for a very long time, holding him, not wanting to hear that horrible, braying laughter. He lay on top of him until the curtain of blackness receded and the world, like the boy beneath him, went quiet, still, and cold. Then Pete cried and shook the boy. "Come back," *he pleaded.* "Please come back."

Sounds from upstairs. Peter pictured the boy in Katy's bed, tiny mouth sucking at her pale breast. He closed his eyes tight, as if that would shut out the noises. Moisture leaked from the corner of his eyes. He felt close to bursting.

Peter stood. An unbearable agony washed through him. He clutched at his stomach, grimaced. He moved to the door, legs unsteady, and out into the night.

Black stars hanging in a cold black sky. A rippling across the dark firmament. Peter rubbed at his wet eyes.

In the barn he lit a small lamp, then sat down, propped against a straw bale. He breathed deep. Hay and sawdust; rotted wood, dry earth, and old sorrows.

Peter blinked. The boy stepped from the shadows into the meagre lamp light. Peter smiled weakly. "You did it," he said. "You came back." Then, inside of him, something swelled and burst into thousands of tiny dark shards. There was a small moment of sudden pain as something spilled out of him, then a cool black nothingness.

He was dimly aware of the boy's tiny figure coming forward, holding a jar. The boy bent to Peter and scooped up dozens of small black stones, pieces of blackness, that lay strewn around Peter. The boy studied the jar, studied Peter, then screwed a lid on the jar, turned and disappeared into the shadows.

The boy was gone. The barn was gone. Katy was gone.

There was nothing but the sky; vast and black and unending.

Then Peter was gone.

A Quiet Axe

Flat lands. Cracked. Heaving. The earth a dry grey tongue. Ghost wisps in the ancient, unsmiling sky. Something finally floating free. A dead thing.

A shack, wind-worn and blanched, boards warped, the wind through the wood singing of madness, like the snap of old bone. Gutters droop under a weighty existence, frowning.

Inside, a man and a woman. He was quick to violence was the man, like a sudden tornado, black and twisted. He'd beat her, and she'd fall, but she couldn't leave. There was nowhere to go. Nothing for miles around but the arid dry land and dusty sky, both ceaseless and unending like her life.

She would think of Becca sometimes, and she'd cry. She couldn't keep it in, not like the man. She'd never seen him cry. He was stoic, dry-eyed, even as his fists preached to her. She wondered if he cried on the inside, if a veil of tears exploded inside his head with each fist-fall, coating his dark skull in a curtain of warm remorse or cold pity. Too much a man to show it. Even that time in the barn, with his singing axe, when he was finished with the stray she'd been feeding, he wore a face of smooth stone. Hers though... hers was a face of sorrows, rutted like the forsaken earth.

Him. Everything inside, bottled up. Nothing leaking out. He'd blamed her, and the land. *Your fault*, he'd said. *Ain't got no call for feeding strays, making them dependent. Can barely feed ourselves. Too many mouths.* Face impassive, his body taut and still as a cobra's before a strike. *The land is a dead thing.* Shaking now. *A dead thing.*

The woman wondered if the man ever thought about Becca. Wondered if he'd ever given her more than a passing thought, or if, in his eyes, she was just another stray. Thoughts of Becca were the only things keeping the woman tethered to this lifeless land. Like the dead, she yearned to be moor-less.

She glanced to the floor, at the man. There was nothing inside him, really, after all. Not anymore. Just a spreading dark wetness, seeping through the floor into the parched and greedy earth.

Outside, the weary sky frowned and the wind murmured of lunacy, like a quiet axe.

Inside, the man gazed upward, dry-eyed and unblinking. The

woman dried her hands in the folds of her dress and squinted through a dirt-smeared window at a barren world. She trembled, blinked, but didn't weep. Not this time. She kept it inside, and it made her buoyant. After a time she went outside and floated away, a ghost of herself.

The Woods

It had been snowing for days. Icy needles of teeth tumbled from the ash-flecked sky, clotted the woods.

The thick shroud of snow shifted, moved with the weeping wind, pushed against a cabin. A bug-bright snowmobile rested near a leaning woodshed like some alien invader, its engine cooling, ticking, though the two men inside the cabin could not hear this. They could hear nothing of the outside world but the wind and its ceaseless winter lament.

Inside, logs crackled and smoldered in a fireplace. A black cast-iron pot hung above the small fire, suspended from a metal rod attached to stanchions. A spicy tang permeated the cabin.

The old man in the old rocking-chair, who had a face like tree bark, blinked crusty eyes, looked up at the younger man (who nonetheless was near retirement himself but was still much younger than the old man in the chair) and gestured to the only other chair in the cabin. "Have a seat, Officer Creed."

The younger man grinned weakly. "How many times I have to tell you, Jack, you don't have to call me that. It's just the two of us. We go back a long way."

The old man blinked again, nodded, stared at the younger man's uniform; the gold badge on the parka, the gun holstered at his side. "Well, Ned," croaked the old man, "it looks like you're out here on business, so it's only proper."

Ned clutched a small, furry, dead animal, fingers digging deep. He sat on the proffered chair, laid the dead thing on the floor, where it resembled a hat. "We go back a long way," he repeated, wistful.

They were silent for a time. The old man rocked slowly and the pine floor creaked. Ned stared at his wet boots, glanced out the window at the swirling sheets of grey-white.

Jack stopped rocking. "Get you some coffee, Ned?"

"No, thanks. Can't stay long. Have to get back before the storm comes full on."

A sad chuckle from the old man. "You may be too late."

"I fear I am, Jack."

Another brief silence ensued. Jack rocked slowly and Ned brushed wet snow from his pants.

"You still trapping?" Ned asked. "Still getting out?"

Jack paused, as if carefully considering his words. "Course I am. I'm old, not dead." Another brief pause, then, "Man's got to eat."

"That's why I'm here."

"I see."

"We go back a long way, don't we, Jack?"

The old man blinked, nodded.

"I mean, you'd tell me if you needed anything, wouldn't you? You'd tell me if anything was wrong?"

The old man leaned forward. "Checking up on me, Ned?"

"You might be snowbound awhile, is all. Just doing my job. You're like a ghost out here."

Jack eased back into the rocker. "Pantry is stocked. Plenty of rabbit in the woodshed."

Ned grimaced. "You were always a good trapper."

"Been here a long, long time, Ned. You do something often enough you get good at it."

"True enough."

"You learn about things," Jack said. "By necessity. You learn how the world works. The good. The bad. All of it."

"Hmm, yes."

"I know things," Jack said. He was staring hard at Ned. "But... tell me, what do you know, Ned?"

Ned fidgeted, returned Jack's look. "Not as much as you, Jack. That's the gospel. I know certain things, that's all. And other stuff I'm not so certain about. Trying to figure things out, is all."

"Oh, you're a sly one, aren't you, Ned?"

Ned turned away, sighed, gazed at the window. "Not so much. No."

"What do you see?" Jack asked.

"I can just make out a few trees. Nothing else. The woods and nothing."

"I know these woods like the back of my hand."

"I bet you do," Ned said.

Gusts of blowing snow swept past the window, a curtain of ice. The cabin door groaned. Each man sat, staring at the other, stealing glances at the window, then the door, expectant, as if waiting for a visitor.

Ned broke the silence. "Tom Brightman's got a spot of trouble."

Jack's face creased into a sneer. "You don't say."

"Wendigo," Ned whispered, as if afraid to say it aloud.

Jack sniggered. "That old saw again?"

"I'm afraid so." Ned scratched his head. "Every year. The same old superstitions. We've heard them all, me and you. We go back some ways."

"Stop saying that."

"It's true, though. There's not much between us. Is there, Jack? There are no secrets in these parts."

"Yes," Jack said.

Ned stretched his legs out, crossed them, uncrossed them. A log in the fireplace popped, split. The room smelled of spice and meat and wet fur. He turned toward the fire.

Jack followed Ned's gaze. "Get you something to eat? To tide you over?"

"No." Ned squirmed. "You hungry, Jack?"

"All the time. Seems the older I get, the hungrier I get." Jack stared off into a far corner. "It's not something I can explain. Not something you'd understand."

Ned gestured to the pot. "Don't mind me. Help yourself."

Jack smirked, swung his gaze around to Ned. "It's okay, I'll wait. I've some manners still."

"You've got a nice little set up out here, Jack. All by yourself. No one around for miles. Must get mighty lonely at times, I'd imagine."

The old man shrugged. "Not really. A man can find plenty of things to occupy his time. Idle hands and all that."

"That's what worries me, Jack. This place, this solitude, this... *nothingness*. It does things to people." Ned leaned forward, nodded toward the window. "You ever spot anything out there, in the woods? Anything... *strange*?"

"Ha." Jack's tree-bark face glowed orange from the fire, a winter pumpkin. "Stealthy man-eating beasts, Ned? Slavering cannibals?

Wendigo?"

Ned blinked, watched Jack, said nothing.

"Tom Brightman is a damn fool," Jack said. "Every year it's the same damn thing. Can't control his dogs so he blames everyone else. Myths. Legends. Old wives' tales. Easier for some men to cast blame than take responsibility."

"What do you know about such things, Jack?"

"How many, Ned? How many of his sled dogs have gone missing this year?"

"None." Ned straightened and leaned forward. Rigid and intent. "It's the youngest boy. Johnny. Been gone a week now."

Jack was quiet. He began to rock slowly. Then, "He's a damn fool."

"May very well be." Ned scratched his chin. "You positive there's nothing I can get you, Jack? Nothing you need?"

"Nothing."

"Don't suppose," Ned asked, "at this point it'd make a lick of difference if I peeked into the woodshed on my way out? To make sure?"

"Not a lick, Ned. Not at this point."

Ned picked up his hat, stood, let out a heavy breath. "That's what I thought." He pulled the hat over his head, went to the door, opened it a crack and peered into the gathering white nothingness. "I'll try and swing by later in the week, Jack. Watch yourself." He shoved through the gap, into the outside, pulled the door shut.

The old man rose from the rocking chair and scuttled across the worn pine floor. He went to the window, pressed his face against the frost-veined pane and spied the younger man, a blurry black smudge, trudging through the blizzard. The younger man stopped at the woodshed, pulled open the door and slipped inside.

Jack watched. Waited. It had been snowing forever. Glassy shards struck the ground, formed an icy shell. He thought surely that the world would crack, that *something* would crack.

Ned exited the shed, paused, gazed back at the cabin, shambled over to his snowmobile. Soon, the white swallowed him.

Jack turned, walked to the cupboards, grabbed a chipped bowl and a spoon, and went over to the fireplace and the pot. Stew bubbled and simmered in the pot. His stomach grumbled, empty, always empty. It wasn't something he could explain. Wasn't something that he understood. A vast emptiness inside him. Nothingness.

He ladled stew into the bowl, spooned the hot meal into his mouth. Chewed. Swallowed. His thoughts turned to Tom Brightman, his dogs, his son... and his daughters.

Jack ate. The emptiness abated. Then he didn't think about anything except the woods.

The woods and nothing.

One Final Breath

"Most fledglings and nestlings won't survive long outside the nest; easy pickings for predators."
- Greta Flemming, "Birding in Your Backyard", Natura Publications (2000)

Sometimes, alone in the quiet night, Miller hears her still. Laughing. Crying. A small whoosh of breath.

As a newborn, Sofie was quick to smile, to laugh. He'd tickle her. He'd blow gently on her face. *"Little bird, little bird. The wind will carry you away,"* he'd say. And Sofie would crinkle her eyes from the sensation, smile, kick her arms and legs and giggle. It got to be a ritual. One of their things. As the months passed and she grew, he'd blow on her face, making her hair wave. *"Don't let the wind carry you away, little bird."* She'd laugh, purse her lips, cheeks puffing, and weakly blow spittle in his face, well pleased at her attempt. And his heart would fill to near bursting. Now it was a broken thing.

And sometimes in the unquiet night he'll wake, sit up, squint into the dark and almost believe he really does see her, Sofie, in that pale green dress he bought her, flitting around like his little bird. See her too-bright, too-big eyes that looked at him with a dark curiosity and intelligence. But Miller will blink, and the apparition will vanish. "Sofie?" he whispers. He strains to hear, but there's nothing but the tick of a wall clock counting off the seconds of his dull life.

"The study, conducted at Ottawa University, deduced that grief, proven to already exacerbate cardiomyopathic conditions ('broken heart disease'), also accelerates and fast-tracks any other underlying medical conditions like cancer, CPD, and infectious diseases."
- Robison Sandler, "Grief Can Kill You", Canadian Journal of Medicine (July 7, 2019)

The dead don't leave us, not really, not ever. Miller knows this. He sees her at night, and he sees her in daylight. He'll turn the corner in the grocery mart, and catch a glimpse of a tiny blonde child, toddling along. Or he'll see her at the park, running after a dog, her coat and hair flying loose and free. He imagines her smile. He imagines the joy in her heart.

The living, though... the living *do* leave. Like Marjorie left. But he couldn't blame her. With Sofie gone, there was nothing left to keep them together. Theirs had been a wounded marriage, and now the stitches had been ripped out. He takes cold comfort with ghosts. Cold comfort with the dead.

> "While economic and societal issues like affordable housing, declining income, and reduced benefits remain key causes of homelessness, segments of society have withdrawn due to various traumas—joblessness; divorce; death of a loved one—that incapacitate."
> - Kelsi Newman (Reuters), "Empathy and Understanding for the Homeless", Chicago Daily News (Nov. 22, 2018)

Miller's colleagues hadn't expected him back so soon, if ever. But Miller had nothing else now, so he was back at his desk after a few Bourbon-fuelled weeks. Not that it mattered; they all avoided him like they would the homeless—no eye contact and a wide berth. As if he didn't exist. Like those other ghosts who haunt the streets, bone-weary and bedraggled, lurching along sidewalks, shivering in doorways, sleeping atop subway grates and cold pavement, their bodies still as a corpse. Miller would prod them sometimes, making sure they were still alive. As if it mattered to anyone. The streets are littered with the dead, the missing, the disappeared.

Now, on the bus, as it trundles and squawks along the gloomy, wet streets, he peers out the grease-smeared windows, looking. Looking for all the things we never see. The dead. Because the dead are memories. And if we don't have memories, we have nothing. But he doesn't see her. Today it's all dark silhouettes slouched over in the heavy rain, each indistinguishable from the other. Formless. Blank. A void. At a stoplight Miller sees a homeless person with a dog huddled in the bus shelter. Sophie had wanted a dog, a puppy. She'd chase after them whenever she spotted one.

"Attempted suicide is like 'a balloon being carried away on a current of grief,' said one patient. 'I was floating free, but still in pain.'"
- Samantha Ortega, "The Search for Answers after Suicide", Wymon University Press (1998)

His second-floor apartment is tiny, cold, and dark, like a coffin. It's enough. It's what he deserves. Downstairs, the dogs are barking. He hears them at night through the thin walls, growling, snapping, barking. He's never seen the dogs, nor the persons in the ground-floor unit, but he can hear them and that makes them real.

Miller goes to the window, pulls aside the flimsy curtain and peers out at the dark street. Again, there's nothing out there. No Marjorie. No Sofie. No packs of snarling dogs. Just the dark. There's always the dark. Like a canvas of black muslin rippling and wavering.

He's suddenly nauseous. Vertiginous, he stumbles to the kitchen sink and retches. Dark droplets spew from his mouth, spatter in the sink, and run blackly down the sides of the stainless-steel bowl. It reminds him of Marjorie's runny black mascara that day. Miller smirks, wipes his mouth with the back of his hand, and stares at the mess. *This is what disease looks like*, he thinks. *Black and cancerous and filling your insides.* Maybe he's sick. Maybe he's dying. That'd be too good for him. He dizzily makes his way to the tattered couch and drops onto it.

Miller blinks. There's a faint noise, a buzz, a thrum. And the couch is vibrating. He rubs his eyes. He must have fallen asleep. The television is broadcasting a soundless white static, but there is still an electrical hum in the air, and he's vibrating, little tingles coursing through him from the couch.

He reaches down, into his back pocket. It's his phone, chirping and buzzing as if alive. He blinks his eyes again, unlocks the phone's screen with a swipe, and puts it to his ear.

"Hullo?"

A staticky thrum and a faint voice that he can't make out.

"Who's there? Marjorie?"

The unintelligible voice grows louder, then recedes to a whisper.

Loud, then quiet. Loud. Now quiet. Shouts, then whispers. Now static—on the phone, on the television, in his head. Miller is crying, sobbing. His body rocks violently.

"Who's there? Who's there? Goddammit, speak to me!" Then there is silence. He thinks the line has gone dead but then, faintly, he hears a child's soft laughter and 'Daddee... daddee.' There is a sharp pain in Miller's chest and his heart thuds loudly in his ears. A *click* and he's been disconnected. He puts down the phone and stares unblinking at the harsh glow of the white static of the dead television. Then another sound: a whimper, a low growl, and the baying of wild dogs.

> "At 1 year of age some toddlers are already verbalizing and mimicking; repeating actions—like dishwashing— and phrases like 'Mommy' or 'Daddy.'
> - Dr. Naomi Steinem, "Developmental Stages of the Newborn", Farcreek Press (2002)

Miller wakes to jaundiced light leaking through his thin curtains, stretching grey tendrils across the room. The television screen is blank and dead. No sounds from outside reach his ears, as if the world is also blank and dead. On the small coffee table, under an inverted glass bowl, is a tiny yellow balloon, shrivelled and pathetic like his heart. Miller stares at it, still not comprehending.

He wonders what time it is. Miller rouses himself from the couch with the intention of getting ready for work but remembers it's the weekend. He's been having trouble keeping track of the days. They bleed from one to the other in a dull fugue. Time, like everything, is a construct.

Miller isn't hungry. He can't remember the last time he ate anything. He is never hungry anymore. There is nothing inside of him except blackness.

He smooths the wrinkles from his shirt, throws on a jacket, shoves his phone in his back pocket, and creeps out the door. He pads down the stairs past the first floor unit—quietly so as not to disturb the dogs—and out the front entrance into the grey day.

Miller glances dry-eyed across the street, into the park. A lone blonde child in a green dress with a yellow balloon stares back at him. He hears a low growl and turns, but there is nothing there. And turns around again to face the park, but it is empty. A faint breeze stirs the swing-set, and leaves scuttle across the patchy ground. He shoves his hands into his pockets and stumbles down the street.

At the street corner, in the doorway of the bakery he and Marjorie used to frequent, there is a homeless person huddled under some sodden cardboard. Miller bends, reaches in and nudges the person. Movement and a grunt. The figure looks up at Miller, blearily. A woman. *Marjorie!?* No, he realises, not Marjorie. The stench of piss and shit and sweat hits him and Miller gags. He retches again, but the blackness stays inside him. Every day he sees them, the disappeared, if not here then in some other doorway, sheltering from society. Still alive, still surviving. Miller fumbles in his pockets for some change, then thinks better of it and steps around the woman and into the shop. He'll buy her a sandwich, some hot soup.

At the take-out counter the shop owner avoids eye contact. Miller can't blame him. He is a pariah, as invisible as the homeless. Soup and sandwich in hand, Miller goes outside but the homeless woman is gone. There isn't even any old cardboard or blankets. Disappeared. As if she'd never been.

Miller starts down the street, toting the bag of food. It smells good, but he still isn't hungry. Nothing stirs in him. The next block over he sees another homeless person huddled and shaking in a doorway. Miller approaches and the man looks up. He recognizes him, yes. The man is scrawny, grey, and unshaven, his hair ragged and unkempt, flopping wildly. Breath rancid. The man coughs black spittle. Miller grins weakly. It is like looking at himself, or someone he once knew. He drops the food and stumbles away, turning a corner.

A short distance down the street sits the Sears store, closed now like many a bygone department store. Miller gapes at it. He totters down to its edifice, to the front door chained and locked. He peers into the shuttered windows, catches vague glimpses of broken mannequins and skeletal racks. He'd bought the dress here—Sophie's first birthday dress. Her only birthday. He'd been so fucking proud of himself, wandering into the children's clothing section and picking out the pale green dress, picturing how it'd look on Sophie. He'd even got the size right. He was a goddam hero. Miller grimaces at the memory, stares at the gaunt face looking back at him from the window. He barely recognizes himself. He needs a shave.

Miller goes to the local corner shop and buys some razor blades. Then he goes to the park and sits on a bench, alone. He wants darkness so he closes his eyes. He thinks about the past few weeks. He'd been reading, and grieving. He read Freud's *Mourning and Melancholia*.

'In mourning it is the world which has become poor and empty; in melancholia it is the ego itself.'

Miller grimaces. Fuck Freud. Fuck everything.

His phone buzzes. Miller opens his eyes, blinks. The park is barren, silent. No barking dogs, no screaming children. He pulls the phone from his pocket, stares at the screen. There is a saved message. He unlocks the screen, presses the message. There's unintelligible babble, then 'Daddee... daddee.' Miller sobs. *Sofie*. Her first words. Marjorie had tried reaching him by phone to tell him. When he didn't pick up, she'd put Sofie on. 'Daddee... daddee.' He'd saved the message. Another moment when his heart had filled to overflowing. He hadn't realized how much being a father would change him.

A gentle breeze stirs, like a small whoosh of breath, and blows warmly across Miller's face. *The wind will carry you away*. A current of grief.

> "The average weight of a 1-year-old boy is 20.8 pounds.
> A girl will average 19.4 pounds—about the weight of
> the average turkey at Thanksgiving."
> - Dr. Naomi Steinem, "Developmental Stages of the
> Newborn", Farcreek Press (2002)

That morning he'd brought home the cake, the decorations, and the dress. Miller remembers their smiles—Marjorie's and Sofie's.

Remembers Sofie flitting around the room in her dress like a little bird as he stuck decorations on the wall. Miller was full of life, buoyant. He felt like he was floating, his life unfolding in a Capra-esque fashion.

Miller was blowing up balloons. Before he tied off each end he'd stop and let the air blow across Sofie's face, ruffling her hair, making her laugh and bounce. '*Fly away, little bird. Fly away.*' He'd leaned over, kissed Sofie gently on the forehead. '*I love you, little bird.*'

Sofie had snatched the yellow balloon in Miller's hand and was trying to blow it up, her cheeks puffing, face reddening. He held the balloon end for her, watched her great effort as she huffed as mightily as she could, the balloon inflating slightly. Miller would pinch off the end so the air didn't escape. Then they had a tiny yellow balloon. Sofie flew around the apartment clutching the balloon end in a tight little fist.

It was his idea to take her to the park. He wanted his little bird to fly. '*You go ahead,*' Marjorie said. '*I'll finish decorating.*'

"Well-known North American breeds like Rottweilers and pit bulls have a bite force of upwards of 300 PSI. European breeds like the Cane Corso and Kangal have a bite force of 700 PSI. All these breeds should be well-trained and socialized before introduction to other dogs and humans."
- Kenneth Dean Haight, "Curbing Canine Aggression: A Practical Guide", Spilo Press (2009)

Miller blinks. It is bright and sunny, the sky a brilliant blue and cloudless. The park is full to bursting with picnickers, children, birds and dogs and squirrels, families, lovers, ice cream and cotton candy vendors, and street performers.

Sofie is chasing a pigeon. She'd insisted on taking her balloon, and it's clutched tightly in one hand. The pale green dress puffs out as she totters after the pigeon. His little bird.

Then Sofie is reaching for the pigeon and the balloon is floating free. It rises up and snags on a branch under the tree canopy. Miller can't reach the small yellow balloon. Squinting against the sun, he spots a knot in the tree and attempts a climb. He's levered himself up close to the balloon when he hears the dogs. He sees them. They are running loose. And Sofie has seen them, too. Laughing, she lurches at them as they race across the field, barking, useless leashes trailing after them. Miller panics. He lets go of the tree, but his shirt has caught on a broken limb, and for what seems an eternity he hangs there hopelessly like a broken marionette, his limbs pinwheeling almost comically. Everything seems to slow and Miller sees her, his tiny bird in a pale green dress as she collides with the dogs.

> "The larger breeds can easily tear apart small animals by latching onto them with their powerful jaws and vigorously shaking their head."
> - Kenneth Dean Haight, "Curbing Canine Aggression: A Practical Guide", Spilo Press (2009)

Miller manages to free himself. He falls, then gets up and sprints towards Sofie, but he's too slow. He can't move fast enough. He hears his heartbeat. He hears barking, snapping, and growling. He sees her caught between them, uncomprehending as they lunge and bite and tear. There's a weak warble above the din of the dogs, and Miller sees the ragged green fabric of the dress, and a gush of crimson. He's moving in slow-motion, and when he gets there it is all a red ruin. Then everything goes dark and silent.

Much later, in a dark fugue, he goes back for the balloon.

Miller blinks again. Everything is dark and silent. He's on the bench in the park and it's night. He doesn't know what time it is. Doesn't care.

He rouses himself and walks across the street to his apartment building. He lets himself in. On the landing he can hear the dogs, whimpering. He hears them at night through the thin walls. He's never seen the dogs, nor the persons in the ground-floor unit, but he can hear them and that makes them real.

In his apartment he sits on the sofa. The little yellow balloon is on his coffee table under a bowl, as if preserved. He lifts the bowl and takes the balloon. It's in there, he knows. Her breath. Sofie's breath. It's in the balloon. It's all he has left.

Miller stands and goes to the bathroom with the balloon. In the medicine chest he finds some sticky gauze tape. He puts a piece of tape on the balloon, then he sits on the edge of the bathtub.

Little bird, little bird. The wind will carry you away.

Miller is crying, but he's calm. He lifts the balloon to his face. He reaches in a pocket for the razor blades he'd bought. He pulls a blade from the case. Carefully, Miller runs the sharp edge atop the tape on the balloon. There's a small whoosh of breath. One final breath.

Then Miller makes another cut. Then another.

And the wind carries him away.

Acknowledgements

Thanks to my family—Carolyn, Courtney, and Daniel—for unwavering love and support.

To David Álvarez for his brilliant cover art, and Vince Haig for his impeccable cover design. And Courtney Kelly for a rigorous edit, and beautiful interior design and layout.

Thanks, as well, to Nathan Ballingrud, Craig Davidson, Brian Evenson, and Paul Tremblay for their generous and kind words about this book.

Finally, thanks to the fine editors who gave these stories good homes: Paul Michael Anderson, Peter Coleborn, Andy Cox, Peter Crowther, Melissa & Michael de Kler, Nick Gevers, Gerard Houarner, Stephen Jones, S.T. Joshi, Nancy Kilpatrick, Mark Leslie, David Longhorn, Sean Moreland, David Morell, C.M. Muller, Joseph S. Pulver Sr., Nicholas Royle, and Simon Strantzas.

About the Author

Michael Kelly is the former Series Editor for the *Year's Best Weird Fiction*. He's a Shirley Jackson Award-winner, and a World Fantasy Award nominee. His fiction has appeared in a number of journals and anthologies, including *Black Static*, *The Mammoth Book of Best New Horror* 21 & 24, *Supernatural Tales*, *Postscripts*, *Weird Fiction Review*, and has been previously collected in *Scratching the Surface*, and *Undertow & Other Laments*.